Love for Dessert

Kate Goldman

Love for Dessert

Published by Kate Goldman

Copyright © 2019 by Kate Goldman

ISBN 978-1-09963-633-2

First printing, 2019

All rights reserved. No part of this book may be reproduced in any form or by any electronic or mechanical means including information storage and retrieval systems – except in the case of brief quotations in articles or reviews – without the permission in writing from its publisher, Kate Goldman.

www.KateGoldmanBooks.com

PRINTED IN THE UNITED STATES OF AMERICA

Dedication

I want to dedicate this book to my beloved husband, who makes every day in my life worthwhile. Thank you for believing in me when nobody else does, giving me encouragement when I need it the most, and loving me simply for being myself.

Table of Contents

CHAPTER 1 1

CHAPTER 2 20

CHAPTER 3 63

CHAPTER 4 86

CHAPTER 5 106

CHAPTER 6 112

CHAPTER 7 129

EPILOGUE 132

WHAT TO READ NEXT? 138

ABOUT KATE GOLDMAN 141

ONE LAST THING..142

Chapter 1

Anastasia Emmott shuffled papers around on her desk aimlessly as she stared out the giant glass windows of the office. The sun was still somewhat bright against a blue summer sky.

Her phone sat beside her computer and she picked it up with one finely manicured hand as she checked the time. Half an hour until her shift was done. It was another boring day at work and Anastasia thanked the heavens that it was Friday.

Lately it seemed like the office was a noose around her neck, suffocating her slowly. Though she had never been a particularly negative person, Anastasia couldn't deny the fact that she was growing to hate her job. Her coworkers had seemed friendly, and they had been at first. That was a year ago. Now, they seemed dull.

They weren't cruel or unusual. It was just that they were so completely and utterly boring. She swore that if she looked up the definition of the word "boring" in a dictionary, their pictures would be next to it. All they did was work, take care of their kids and maybe play golf on the weekends. For a twenty-five-year-old like Anastasia, they and their kind of life didn't look very appealing. Though her cubicle was pretty big for her position, and she made enough to get by comfortably, she craved excitement and something different almost every day.

Her phone rang quietly. The caller ID read Ariana Clemens, Anastasia's best friend. She looked around to make sure no one was watching her take a personal call. She was glad to see that everyone was busy staring at their computers or chatting among themselves. "Hey Ari, what's up?"

"You will not guess what happened! You need to come over tonight. I'll tell you *all* about it." Anastasia grinned. Typical Ariana. Her excitement was always infectious, and Anastasia loved it. Ariana had always been like this, ever since they had been small children.

"Alright, alright. I will. I'm off in half an hour, I'll head there immediately, okay?"

"Mmkay! See you soon!" A quiet click told Anastasia that Ariana had hung up. That was Ariana, never a dull moment.

Anastasia sat back in her comfy black chair, playing with a strand of her light golden hair as she wondered what Ariana's great news was. Her phone buzzed, letting her know she had a text. Ah, it was Aaron. Aaron Rose was Anastasia's boyfriend of three years. They had met while she was at college, and had been together ever since. His dark brown hair and twinkling blue eyes attracted her to him almost the moment she laid eyes on him. She was almost certain that this was the man she was supposed to be with for the rest of her life. And he seemed to feel the same.

How's work? The text read. *I'll be home earlier tonight, so I'll make or bring dinner. C U.* Aaron used to text her with smiling faces and sweet words, but Anastasia pushed her feelings of insecurity deep down into her heart. They were in love. And he would propose one day, right? Anastasia sighed as she texted back that she would be home after Ariana's.

The next half an hour sped by as she attempted to work, but found herself constantly distracted, thinking about Ariana's news. She remembered her mother had tried getting her diagnosed for ADD because she was so easily distracted, but had finally come to the conclusion that Anastasia was just different and her mind worked in different ways.

Anastasia's mother, Erica Emmott, was indeed something else. She had already been married five times, and was soon about to go on her sixth. Erica was always telling Anastasia that she needed to find a man, to get settled down. And after Anastasia found Aaron, she didn't stop there. She just kept saying that Aaron needed to propose. Just thinking about her gave Anastasia a migraine.

Anastasia opened her email inbox, and saw there was an email from her mother sitting there. Speak of the devil… The subject title read *ANASTASIA!* in all capital letters and a loud exclamation mark. That sounded like trouble but Anastasia clicked it anyway. She scanned it quickly, taking in her mother's irritated words, telling her that she needed to visit and it had been ages since she had last. In actuality though, it had only been a couple days.

Thankfully, Anastasia's phone beeped, letting her know that it was time to clock out. She grabbed her phone and bag, and headed out as quickly as possible. She breathed in the fresh air of Chicago, happy to be free for the night. It was easy to get a taxi and she headed towards Ariana's place.

As soon as Anastasia reached the apartment that Ariana shared with her boyfriend Peter Gold, she knocked on the door, excited. "Hey!" Ariana called happily as she opened the door. "Come in, come in."

"So, what's the big news? Spill it!" Anastasia collapsed onto the sofa as Ariana smiled coyly. Ariana's adorable features made her look like a child and her flaming red hair seemed like something out of a cartoon. She had freckles on both cheeks, something she had been self-conscious about but with Anastasia's help had gotten over.

"It's about Peter..." Ariana giggled. "He proposed!" she exclaimed as Anastasia let out a squeal of surprise.

"Oh my God! Show me the ring!" Ariana held out her left hand and there it was, the big sparkling diamond. "That's gorgeous!" Anastasia felt a pang of jealousy but she pushed it away. It truly was a beautiful piece of jewelry, and it showed very clearly just how much Peter loved Ariana.

"Will you be my maid of honor, Ana?" Anastasia nodded happily as she oohed and aahed appropriately over the incredibly expensive rock. "So, Ana," Ariana started after the initial surprise had passed, "when is Aaron going to pop the question?"

Anastasia sat back into the sofa and picked at her perfectly manicured nails nervously, unsure how to answer the question. "I guess sometime soon. I'm sure he will though…" she said in a wistful tone. She couldn't deny the seeds of envy that grew within her heart, for she didn't want to admit that it looked like Aaron was never going to propose.

"Don't worry, Ana, I'm sure he'll propose soon! Then I can help you plan your wedding!" Ariana was endlessly optimistic, and Anastasia was glad that Ariana didn't notice that anything was wrong. She didn't want to talk about it at all. The rest of the visit passed uneventfully, and Anastasia had a fun time discussing wedding plans with Ariana.

She returned home around six, looking forward to seeing Aaron. She turned her keys in the lock and opened the door, feeling relaxed the second she saw the familiar sights of her own apartment. A lovely aroma was in the air and Anastasia was certain that Aaron was making something delicious. "I'm home, darling!" she called happily. Anastasia walked into the kitchen, dropping all her things on a chair beside the table. "What's cooking?"

"Just soup." Aaron was wearing a plain white apron, stirring something in a big silver pot. "Welcome home." She kissed him on the cheek as she grabbed white bowls out of the cupboard. "It's almost done. Thanks."

Aaron looked good today, and Anastasia liked it. She could smell his signature scent as she wrapped her arms around him and gave him a hug. "You smell nice." She kissed his neck tenderly. Usually, this was Aaron's favorite move of hers.

Aaron didn't say anything, and merely ladled the soup into the bowls. "Let's eat."

She was hoping he would compliment her, or say he loved her, or show any sort of affection, but he didn't. Anastasia pressed her lips together as she sat down and began to eat her soup. "This is good."

Aaron smiled awkwardly.

Anastasia continued to attempt to make conversation. "So, you remember what is in two weeks, right?" She grinned happily.

"Our anniversary, right?" Aaron hoped he was right, because he honestly didn't know.

"Yep! I was thinking of going out to dinner… Just a small celebration. What do you think?" Anastasia picked at her soup. Aaron had forgotten that she didn't like onions. Again.

"Yeah, sure, that sounds good…" he said in a quiet tone. He was tired, yes, but recently, to him, their relationship had seemed like one big bothersome thing that stood in his path. He loved Anastasia, he truly did, but he felt like they just weren't the right fit for each other.

Anastasia wasn't the type of person to point out things that were wrong. She lived by the motto "ignorance is bliss." So she kept her mouth shut. *He's just tired from a long day at work, right?* she thought, hoping it was true.

"I'm done," he said as he brought his bowl to the sink, and dropped it loudly. Anastasia sighed as she picked at her soup, her appetite suddenly lost. She forced herself to finish the rest of the food as she washed the bowls and put them away. Anastasia had grown into the role of housewife, and sometimes she wondered if Aaron took her for granted.

She headed into their shared bedroom, where she found Aaron using his laptop at the desk. "Hey," she said.

He didn't even look up. "Hi."

Judging by his response, he wasn't too enthusiastic to be talking to her but she brushed it off and continued on. "So, Ariana's getting married... Peter proposed. Isn't it wonderful?" she said as she moved closer to her boyfriend, wrapping her arms around his neck. She planted a kiss on his cheek.

"I suppose," he said as he kept his eyes trained on the bright screen.

Clearly, Aaron wasn't getting Anastasia's hints about marriage. "Do you think we'll be like them?" she tried again, more obvious this time.

"Maybe."

Anastasia moved her hands downwards towards Aaron's crotch area, her intentions clear to him. She wanted a reaction out of him, or something more than a couple one-word responses but she wasn't going to get it. "Ana, I'm busy, not now, okay?" Aaron had never been one to turn down sex and this surprised Anastasia more than anything.

"Alright... I'm going to bed then," Anastasia muttered, her heart heavy. "Goodnight."

And that was that.

Love for Dessert

***

Anastasia woke up in the morning to an empty apartment. She sighed as the reality hit her, that Aaron wasn't loving towards her, she felt completely alone, and that she felt like their relationship had an expiration date. But still, she had an appearance to keep up. One of a happy relationship, a perfect home.

So she ran a comb through her hair, brushed her teeth, put her makeup on. In the mirror, she looked bright and happy, nothing like what she felt. She plodded with her fuzzy slippers to the kitchen, where she found a note on the table.

Anastasia—

We need to talk. I'll be home at two.

Her hands began to shake as she clutched the small sheet of paper. Those initial four words... They meant so much though they were but simple ones. Her mouth grew dry as she licked her suddenly dry lips. "This can't be happening..." she moaned quietly as she looked at the kitchen clock. One forty-five. It wasn't enough time for her to mentally prepare. And now she realized with a pang that she was preparing for the worst.

Anastasia made herself a warm cup of tea as she sat down at the kitchen table, and waited for Aaron to come home. Time ticked by slowly like mud as she waited. The key turned in the door at two fifteen, and

Love for Dessert

Anastasia's heart began to beat like mad. She didn't turn her head to look at him, but she heard him come in and drop his keys into the bowl. She heard the telltale sound of his bag falling to the floor. "Hi," he said in his familiar voice and for a heartbeat, she believed everything was normal.

"Hi…" she breathed out.

"Did you get my note?"

She nodded timidly.

He dragged a chair dragged across the floor loudly and took a seat. "Anastasia… I can't do this anymore. I've been lying to you."

"About what?" Anastasia's voice was quiet. If it wasn't too bad a thing, she would forgive him. It's what people in relationships did. They forgave and they moved on. That's what she believed.

"I'm not in love with you anymore," he mumbled so softly as drops of water gathered at the corner of his eye. It was painful seeing the look on her face, and he still loved her, though he no longer wanted to be romantically involved with her for the rest of his life.

Anastasia couldn't even cry, she just sat there, frozen. It would have been better if he had just stabbed her in the heart. She felt stunned, and unable to even say anything.

"I'm sorry, Anastasia. We're too different." He raised a hand and wiped away a tear. "Please. Say something."

"I… I can change." Her voice quivered and sounded so completely weak as she spoke. "Please, Aaron, don't leave me." Anastasia's greatest fear was being alone. And now, it was staring her in the face, all too real, all too fast. "I'll do anything."

"I'm sorry, Anastasia, I've already made up my mind." Aaron shook his head, defeated, as he closed his eyes and tried to blink back his tears. This was breaking his heart, but nearly not as much as he was breaking hers.

Anastasia felt the all too familiar sting in her nose as tears began to well up. She wasn't sure what to say. She wanted to yell at him, to call him an asshole, to scream other profanities in his face but there was no use. She was going to be alone. "Aaron… Did I mean nothing to you? Don't you love me?" She was completely aware of how pathetic she must have looked and sounded, but she didn't care. If it would make him stay, it would be worth every shred of her pride that she shed.

"I… I'll be out by the end of the week." Aaron slid his chair back and stood up. His face was emotionless as he turned his eyes away from her. She looked so broken, sitting there, her face in her hands. He didn't want to cry in front of her. It would only make things harder.

She waited until she heard the slamming of the bedroom door before allowing herself to succumb to the tears. Her body was wracked with sobs as she felt the weight of the world crash onto her shoulders. All these years, she had worked so hard to please Aaron, to make sure that he was happy, but it seemed like nothing she did helped. She cried as she poured herself a glass of wine, determined to drown out her thoughts.

She drank glass after glass until she decided that it was useless to keep pouring herself new ones for she was eventually going to drink the entire thing anyway. Anastasia fell asleep with the bottle in her arms, her makeup running down her face in disarray.

***

Pain.

That was all Anastasia could feel, mentally and physically. Her head pounded as she regretted drinking so much the night before. But she wasn't cold, there was a blanket wrapped around her. Aaron was the only person who could have put it on her, and it hurt to realize that he still cared about her. She would rather have him hate her, that way it would be much less painful.

Love for Dessert

The warm comforter still smelled like him and she pulled it in towards her nose, breathing in his familiar smell. It comforted her, yet brought on a fresh wave of tears as she realized that within a couple of weeks, she would never be able to feel this delicious scent fill her nose again.

"I miss you," she murmured out quietly, to no one at all. She knew he couldn't hear her, and was probably already out. She forced herself to get up, to check the bedroom, and just as she thought, he wasn't there. Her eyes scanned across the now somewhat empty room, and realized that Aaron had already taken most of his clothes. He had been planning this for weeks. And she had missed every sign.

He had left a couple winter jackets in the closet, and she brushed her nose across them; the scent made her feel like he was still there, holding her in his arms. She collapsed onto the bed, and fell into a deep, dreamless sleep.

***

Anastasia woke up to the familiar sound of her ringtone echoing loudly throughout the small apartment. It was darker outside, and Anastasia guessed it to be around four in the afternoon. It was her mother. *Damn it.* "Hello?" she answered quietly, praying that her mother couldn't detect what a state she was in.

Love for Dessert

But Erica Emmott was no fool. "What's wrong? You sound depressed." She knew her daughter well. "C'mon, spill."

Anastasia knew there was no point in lying. "Aaron left me," she mumbled as the weight of it all hit her, and tears crept from her eyes. She felt like a child, sobbing on the phone to her mother.

"Oh, Ana, honey…" Erica's voice immediately slipped into a motherly tone as she worried about her daughter. "Do you want me to come over?" Erica sighed as she listened to Anastasia cry. "I'm coming over."

Anastasia heard the phone click and she was too depressed to protest. She was just grateful her mother had not said "I told you so." That seemed to be Erica's favorite phrase, and Anastasia hated it. Erica had always told her that men were trouble, but it always seemed so hypocritical because Erica herself had been married so many times.

Erica had her own key to Anastasia's apartment, and was there a quick half an hour later, for she had screamed at the taxi driver to drive as quickly as possible. She had brought a tub of ice cream, Anastasia's favorite flavor, green tea. She opened the door to the quiet apartment. All the lights were off, and Erica couldn't hear a single sound. "Ana? Darling?" There was no answer. Erica pushed open the door to the bedroom and discovered a lump underneath the bed covers. She realized that the closet door was slightly ajar, and she could see that it was mostly empty. *Ah, Aaron's gone already...* Erica sighed.

"Mom?" Anastasia's voice sounded feeble and unlike her.

"Hi, honey." Erica moved closer and took a seat on Anastasia's bed. Her normally beautiful daughter looked disheveled and tired.

Anastasia sat up as she took in her mother's appearance. Erica wore a flashy red dress that was ten years too young for her, and her makeup was outrageous. Erica always dressed to impress the next poor sucker who would marry her and Anastasia knew this well. "You look well, mom," she muttered. "Is that ice cream?"

"Yes, and I brought spoons. But really, I've always told you, that boy was trouble." Erica wasted no time in telling Anastasia what she had done wrong. "Eat this. Oh lord, you smell terrible. When was the last time you showered? And your breath!"

Anastasia glared at her mother. "Mom, I've been really upset."

"That's no excuse, Ana." Erica gave Anastasia a stern look as she set the tub of ice cream aside and pulled her daughter in for a warm hug. "It'll be alright. Don't worry."

Anastasia sunk into her mother's hug as tears filled her eyes once more. "I never thought he'd leave me…" she cried desperately. "We were supposed to be together… forever…" She mumbled as she tasted salt. "I love him so much…"

Erica's heart broke along with Anastasia's as she watched her daughter crumble in her arms. "Shh… It'll be okay…" She mumbled comforting words as she pressed her lips together in a thin line. Truth be told, she had had quite a good feeling about Aaron, and was incredibly disappointed that it hadn't worked out.

Anastasia cried for so long, by the time the clock turned five thirty, she felt like she was out of tears to cry. Her heart hurt, but her mother's comforting embrace was something she had missed. "Thanks, Mom," she murmured. "I should clean up."

"Good girl." Erica smiled. "Now, are you going to be alright, or should we go for dinner together?"

"I'll be fine… I'll just get some takeout. You can go home." Anastasia smiled. She was determined to be strong. She had a life outside of Aaron after all.

Erica thought about it. "Alright, I should be heading back soon anyway, I think George wanted to see me tonight." Anastasia didn't even bother to ask. George was probably her mother's new beau and knowing

Erica, he'd be tall, handsome and rich. Erica frowned. "Aren't you even going to ask who he is?"

"Nope." Anastasia laughed.

"It's nice to see you smile, darling. I'll see you soon, call me, okay?" Erica wrapped her stylish black trench coat around her dress, and walked out of the apartment into the hallway, her much too high heels clattering on the floor.

Anastasia heaved a sigh as she watched her mother walk away. She was alone again, but this time, she didn't feel so lonely. She had to tell Ariana the bad news, but she couldn't stand the pity. She hated people feeling sorry for her, for she was so prideful. She decided she would tell Ariana tomorrow. And it was Monday again, which meant work.

Anastasia fixed herself dinner, and then headed towards her bed, where she would stay for the rest of the night.

***

The alarm clock rang loudly in the morning; Anastasia grumbled as she hit snooze, getting up. It was a new day, and she felt refreshed. Life would go on. She headed to work, and sat in her cubicle, like she always did. The incessant chatter of her coworkers started. Usually, Anastasia didn't pay attention, but this time, it was different.

"Hey, Anastasia, did you hear?" One of her coworkers, a gossip named Reina, leaned over from her own cubicle. "A bunch of workers are getting demoted or laid off. And the demoted ones… They earn practically nothing."

"That's terrible!" Anastasia looked shocked as she hoped she wasn't one of them.

"Check your email. It's important!" Reina went back to her own cubicle as Anastasia did what she was told, and opened her email.

There was an email from her boss sitting at the top of her unread messages, and the subject line read "important." Uh-oh. That seemed ominous. Anastasia clicked it open, not sure what to expect. She scanned the email, and realized with a pang that she was one of those who were to be demoted. And it was like Reina had said, their salary was tiny.

Fueled with anger, Anastasia's heart pounded in her ears as she glared angrily at her screen. She couldn't believe this was happening. These past years, she had worked long and hard for this firm, and now they were demoting her to such a terrible position.

First Aaron, then this. Anastasia had had it with all the bad luck in her life and she was taking charge. Adrenaline coursed through her body as she stood up with determination and stalked towards her boss' office. She knocked, loudly, then waited for his response. "Come in!" he called loudly.

"Hello…" she said as she pushed open the door and saw her boss, sitting behind his table. He was a big fellow.

"Ah, Anastasia, did you get my email?" Anastasia grumbled as she noted how annoying his face looked for the first time. Her boss grinned as if he didn't know how mad she was. "What's wrong?"

Anastasia summoned all of her strength as she uttered the next words: "I quit."

Chapter 2

"What are you going to do now?!" Erica Emmott was relentless as she scolded Anastasia. "How could you have been so silly, quitting your job like that!" Erica sighed heavily as she glared at her daughter, who shriveled under her piercing gaze. "Are you crazy? Is this because of Aaron? Really, Anastasia, I raised you better than this!"

"Mom, they were going to demote me!" Anastasia tried to argue back. "And it's only been a week since Aaron left… Why can't you support me? I no longer want to be a stuffy accountant, it's tedious! I need change in my life."

"Other women get a new haircut or a pet or something, but quitting your career job? Really! I can hardly believe it." Erica frowned in disappointment.

"Well, believe it, Mom. Because it's happened." Anastasia rolled her eyes.

Erica sighed. "So what are you going to do now? Become a fairy tale princess?"

Anastasia picked up the newspaper that was lying on the kitchen table. She pointed at a leasing advertisement for an empty space in the city. "Open a bakery."

Love for Dessert

***

It took a while to calm Erica down, but nearly an hour later, Anastasia managed to succeed. "Honey, I know you've always wanted to be a baker, but it's not a practical idea!"

"No, Mom, it's all going to work out! Don't worry. I'm going to go check out the open place in half an hour. It would mean a lot to me if you supported me. Please, Mom?" Anastasia shot her mother a pleading look.

"Fine... Honey, if this is really what you want to do, then I support you to the best of my ability." Erica sighed. "I'll even come with you today, how about that?"

"Thanks, Mom." Anastasia grinned. "It's nice of you to offer, but Ariana and I are going together. She'll be here any minute now."

Erica nodded understandingly. "Alright, alright. I'll get out of your hair then." She picked up her bags and after a nice hug, headed out the door.

Ariana arrived a couple minutes later, in a clean summer dress and an adorable pink bag. "Hey, girl!" Anastasia greeted her. "Ready to go?"

"Yep, let's go!"

***

Anastasia spun around happily, her arms out in the air. "This is perfect!" The place had originally been a café, and it was absolutely amazing. It was a quaint little space, and all it needed was a new paint job and some furniture. She could see it now, her bakery would be cute yet elegant. "Ariana, isn't this just fabulous?"

Ariana laughed hesitantly. "Yeah, Ana, it's real nice and all, but the thing is… There's another bakery right over there." She pointed across the street, a couple shops away. "There's going to be a lot of squabbling over business…"

"Hmm…" Anastasia thought about it. "Maybe we should go over to check them out. See how their business is."

"Are you still any good at baking?" Ariana said as she swatted Anastasia on the arm playfully. "I've never eaten anything you've made in ages."

Anastasia didn't miss a beat. "Yes you have. Remember your birthday cake, when I wouldn't tell you where I got the cake from? The one you ate almost half of?" She pointed at herself proudly.

"What! Really?!" Ariana laughed happily. "Then, damn, you got skill. I'm convinced. Now let's head over there."

Ariana and Anastasia headed over to the other bakery. It looked a little old-fashioned, and they weren't too surprised to see an older man standing behind the counter. "Hello," he said, and smiled kindly.

"Hello!" They greeted him warmly as they browsed the selection. The bakery had croissants, and some other assorted old-fashioned pastries.

"There's only one other person in here…" Ariana whispered in a quiet voice, not wanting to offend the man.

Anastasia shrugged. "Maybe it's a slow day."

"Ah, Darren!" The old man exclaimed suddenly. The two girls watched as a younger man walked in through the back. "Welcome back."

"Thanks." His voice was deep, and masculine, and sent shivers down Anastasia's spine. She couldn't see his face, but she could see that he was tall, incredibly so, and he was well built, like he worked out regularly. He didn't look like the typical man who worked at a bakery.

Before Anastasia could get a glimpse of him, her phone rang. It was the real estate agent. "Hello?" she answered as she motioned to Ariana that they should go back across the street. "Uh-huh… I see… Yes, I'll be right there…"

"What was that all about?" Ariana asked as Anastasia hung up.

"Someone else is also interested in the place. Damn it. Should I take it?" she said as they walked back towards the empty place.

"I say do it. Be a little spontaneous. You need the change and fresh start, especially after…" Ariana stopped and pulled Anastasia in for a hug, not wanting to mention Aaron's name. "It'll work itself out."

"Thanks, Ari. You're the best. Really." Anastasia pushed open the door of the empty place. "Regina?"

Regina the real estate agent came out of the back almost immediately, holding a clipboard and a pen. "Will you take it?" She smiled brightly, hoping to make the sale.

Anastasia gave Ariana one last glance before turning back to Regina. "Yes."

***

The next few weeks were filled with excitement, as Anastasia prepared for her bakery's grand opening. There were things to buy, ingredients to order, flyers to be put up, advertisements to be designed, oh, there was just so much work to do. Anastasia was glad for all the work, because it helped her keep her mind off Aaron.

Ariana's wedding plans were also coming along quite nicely, for she had hired an expert wedding planner who took care of her every need. She had picked out the perfect white dress, and even a beautiful outfit for the bridesmaids. Everything was going along smoothly, and Ariana and Peter seemed more in love than ever.

Anastasia was happy for her best friend, but she couldn't help but feel something was missing from her own life. A man. She was beginning to get over Aaron, and it was easier because the last couple months with him had felt one-sided anyway. Anastasia stood outside of her bakery, thinking of a name. It had to be something creative, yet tasteful…

She thought about it as she closed up the bakery, glad that in a couple weeks' time, it would finally be opening. Erica had finally come around, offering financial and emotional assistance, and without her mother, the bakery would have been hard to make a reality. And now it was really happening. Anastasia could hardly believe it, and she was incredibly excited.

Anastasia had a sudden desire to celebrate, but she knew that Ariana was meeting with her wedding planner and she definitely did not want to go drinking with her mother. So she headed to the nearest bar, ironically named Poison, for a drink before going home.

Love for Dessert

Poison was a rather popular bar with the older crowd, and Anastasia didn't usually go there; she and Ariana more often frequented Lights, a bar that had pulsating neon lights and a top 100 playlist. But today, Anastasia was feeling something more low-key. She stepped through the wooden doors, feeling relaxed immediately by the calming piano music and dim lights. There weren't too many people here, and that's how she liked it.

Anastasia took a seat at the bar, and ordered. "A gin and tonic, please."

"Coming right up." The bartender was a pretty woman, and she made the drink quickly and expertly. It was obvious many of the men at the bar were only there to stare at her. The bartender had no problems with this, and her low-cut top earned her more tips than the other drink mixers.

"Thanks." Anastasia shot her a smile as she took a sip of the drink. She surveyed the room, feeling the alcohol travel down her throat satisfyingly. It had been a while since she had had a reason to celebrate, and it felt good. She was finally realizing her childhood dream. Though she still had many hurdles to jump over, financially and emotionally, she had a feeling that everything was going to work itself out. There was a sense of calmness in the entire place, and she enjoyed it. There was a couple in the corner, touching each other intimately, thinking they couldn't be seen underneath the dim lights. Anastasia chuckled.

There was a clunk next to her and Anastasia turned her head to see that a handsome man had moved to the stool next to her at the bar. He was drinking whiskey, straight, and was wearing a smart suit. Damn, he looked good. Anastasia licked her lips as she looked him up and down. He had long legs, and a chiseled body, like a Greek god. His suit hung off his body well, outlining all of his assets.

The mysterious stranger lifted his glass to his lips as he moved his stool closer to hers. "Have we met?" His voice was deep, and sent tremors down her spine.

She was taken aback, for it seemed like he was hitting on her and if he was, then it would be the first time in ages. "I don't think we have…" She smiled coyly as she traced the rim of her cup with a finely manicured finger. It was obvious that he liked what he saw, and she felt the same. It had been a while since she had felt that tingling in her stomach for a man.

"Christopher Myers."

He stretched out a hand and she took it. "Anastasia Emmott."

"Beautiful name. And beautiful blue eyes."

Oh, he was a smooth one and she liked it. Anastasia smiled sweetly as she flipped her blond hair behind her shoulder and leaned onto her left shoulder, locking her eyes onto his dark black ones. She wasn't going to lie, he looked like trouble but trouble always came with a little fun. And fun was exactly what she needed.

"Thanks… You're not so bad-looking yourself." She winked before turning back to her drink.

"So what's a pretty lady like you doing all alone on a gorgeous night like this?" His smile was dazzling, showing all his pearly white teeth. She guessed that he was a businessman, or a lawyer. Whatever he was, it seemed to be a good profession.

Anastasia sipped her gin and tonic. "Just enjoying a drink before I head back to my apartment…" she murmured, tapping her nails on the bar.

"Well, I see you're almost done with your drink, allow me to buy you another."

Ah, yes, this Christopher Myers fellow was the perfect gentleman. Anastasia was quickly taken in by his bright smile and his charming words. Within the hour, they were both in his car, speeding back to his apartment. She knew it was a stupid move, and that she knew better than to go with a stranger but he was just so sexy and everything that came out of his mouth made her want to tear his shirt off and take him in her arms.

"We're almost there…" He chuckled as he placed a hand on hers, which was resting on her leg. She turned her head and watched as he winked at her.

He pulled into a parking garage and wrapped an arm around her as they walked to the elevator. The doors slid open, and they stepped inside. The second the metal doors shut, Christopher pushed her against the wall and pressed his hot, eager lips to hers. He licked her lips with his tongue as her lips parted. Their tongues entwined as her eyes pressed firmly shut, feeling him move against her.

A moan escaped her lips as she felt something hard press against her body. "Someone's excited." She laughed throatily as he pulled away and sucked deeply on her neck, leaving a bright red mark. His free hand traveled up her leg and was reaching for the sensitive spot between her legs when… *Ding!*

They had reached their floor.

"Wait just a minute longer…" he whispered as he pulled away from her and she ran her hands through her hair, straightening it. The doors opened, and they stepped out onto a nice lush carpet. He smiled at her once before directing her towards a door a couple steps away. He pulled out a key and unlocked the door to his apartment. As soon as she walked in, she was engulfed by a light flowery scent. It was a weird thing to smell in a man's home, but as the lights flickered on, Anastasia found that there was an abundance of flowers. His apartment was otherwise tastefully decorated. Were the floral arrangements from admirers?

"I like flowers," he said lightheartedly. "Would you like a glass of wine?"

"That sounds lovely." She smiled.

He kissed her on her cheek as he motioned towards the comfy looking sofa. "Take a seat, I'll bring it out."

Minutes later, he came out carrying two wine glasses, filled halfway with a dark crimson liquid. "Here you go, Anastasia."

"Thank you." She smiled as she removed her shoes, and curled up onto the sofa. He sat down next to her, set his own glass down onto the coffee table and took his jacket off, revealing his crisp white shirt. He untied his tie, draping it delicately over the sofa arm.

The two sat and talked only for a couple minutes, as they both drained their glasses of the alcoholic liquid. By this time, Anastasia was somewhat intoxicated, and could only focus on the handsome man in front of her, talking softly in that low, sexy voice.

"Why don't we… move this to the bedroom?" he murmured quietly. His eyes were absolutely dreamy and seemed to cast a magic spell over her.

Anastasia nodded and allowed him to take her into the darkened bedroom, where a large king-sized bed covered with plush pillows stood in the center. As soon as they were plunged into the darkness, he brushed his lips along her neck and pushed her onto the bed. She fell with a loud thump onto the padded covers as he clambered onto her.

"Mm, you smell delicious…" he whispered as he left a trail of kisses along her jawline, leaving her breathless. She knew this wasn't a good idea, but a part of her desperately wanted this to happen; she needed more excitement in her life. Anastasia smiled as she felt his erection eagerly press against her leg. Her top slipped off easily, and fell to the floor. It was soon joined by her figure-hugging skirt, and her black lace-fringed underwear. Passion was all she felt as he sucked on her breast. She moaned as his hands set her on fire. It had been too long since she had been touched like this.

Oh, she felt like she had been dead for so many years, and was finally coming alive. As Christopher took her, she relished in the fact that this was a man who wanted her and was completely attracted to her. "You're so amazing…" he moaned as he moved into her. She smiled as she took in his words. But a small nagging voice in her head told her that he was only saying these things because she was sleeping with him; she pushed it aside.

As he brought her to her climax over and over again that night, Anastasia floated into a state of pure ecstasy. This was where she was meant to be, she thought.

And for the first time in a long time, Anastasia truly felt like a woman again.

***

The morning felt perfect. The sun was bright in the sky, it was nice and warm in the room, and the bedsheets were soft and comfortable. Except... Anastasia turned over to kiss Christopher good morning and discovered she was alone. "Christopher?" she called as she got out of bed and slipped on her underwear and shirt. When there was no response, she headed out of the bedroom into the living room. "Christopher...?"

Anastasia entered the kitchen, grabbed a glass and was drinking tap water when she noticed a small note on the table. "Huh?" she murmured as she moved closer and sat down, reading it. *Thanks for last night. It was fun.* And that was all it said. He signed off with a needlessly large and exaggerated C. Anastasia pursed her lips as she grabbed the pen beside the note and wrote down her number.

She had to go meet Ariana for lunch, and they would discuss the name of the bakery. It was the last touch before opening, for everything else had already been arranged. Anastasia pulled on her skirt, feeling a little odd that she was wearing the clothes from last night, and headed out the door, hoping Christopher would call. It had been quite the night, and he was an excellent lover. She reached her apartment rather quickly, and ran into the shower as soon as she entered the door. Anastasia picked out a loose black blouse and a summery skirt and put them on. She did her makeup, and grabbed her favorite purse before heading out to meet Ariana.

Aaron had come while Anastasia was out of the apartment and cleaned out his things ages ago, and she was glad that there was no longer any reminder of him in her apartment. She had finally moved on, though her heart was still scarred by the enormous pain he had inflicted. She was smarter now, and knew that she would never wait for a man to change.

Ariana and Anastasia headed to a lovely little café near Ariana's apartment, one they frequented. "So, what kind of names did you have in mind?" Ariana asked.

"I haven't been able to think of any." Anastasia grimaced as Ariana laughed loudly.

"Oh, Ana, don't worry. I'm good at this. How about… Cookie Crumble?" Anastasia shook her head. "Hmm… What about using your name? Ana's Delights."

"That's not a bad idea… Ana's Sweets!" Anastasia lit up happily. "That sounds pretty good, right?"

Ariana grinned. "It's perfect." Their food arrived and they began to eat, both happy. "So the opening is in three weeks, right? Damn, that's soon. Can't believe it's all gone by so fast…"

"I can't believe it either, Ari. I'll just let the sign makers know. We still need to make flyers or something, to get the word out." Anastasia pressed her lips together in a thin line, a trait she inherited from her mother, as she thought.

"Oh, I know the perfect thing! It's a baking contest, and it's happening the week after next. I heard the winner gets thousands of dollars, and a news story done on them! It'd be the perfect opportunity. And I know you're good enough!" Ariana's eyes lit up in excitement as she pulled the advertisement out of her bag. "Here, read!

Anastasia grinned. "This looks good. Thanks, Ari."

The rest of the afternoon consisted of Anastasia and Ariana making final decisions about the bakery, and ordering adorable furniture. Ariana was a real help during the entire process, with her business mind. They had picked out a theme. They were going with the classic sweets café look, and it would look just perfect. The bakery across the street was advertised just as a bakery, so since theirs had a unique twist, they figured it would help bring in customers.

Christopher didn't call.

Love for Dessert

***

Anastasia got home late, around eight, and she was tired. She dropped her bags off as usual and logged onto the computer, making her way over to the baking contest's website. She signed up quickly, glad that the signup was still open. The requirements were that she make a dessert. It was probably a good idea to learn a new recipe, one that would knock the judges' socks off, and she had two weeks to do so.

There was a list of contenders, and she scanned the list, looking for her top competition. There weren't many names that she recognized, and she figured most of them were like her, starting up a bakery.

She checked her phone, and found that there was still no message from Christopher. Slightly disappointed, she poured herself a glass of wine and reminisced about the night they had shared. Anastasia sighed as she decided to go to bed early tonight, and perhaps he would call in the morning.

***

Anastasia awoke in the morning with a smile on her face. She had dreamt that she was getting married, to the perfect man of her dreams, though she couldn't see who it was. Nevertheless, it left her in a happy mood. She dressed hurriedly and headed off to the bakery. The sign makers had sent her an email, letting her know that they were putting in the sign today.

Love for Dessert

Ariana had promised Anastasia that she would take care of the design. Ariana was a rather talented artist.

She stood at the curb as she watched them pull out the sign, covered in cloth. It took them a while, but they managed to affix it to the front of her restaurant. "Can I see it?" she asked one of them.

"Of course." He moved and pulled the cloth away grandly. She gasped. It was perfect. There was an expertly drawn portrait of Anastasia smiling gleefully beside the swirling words that read *"Ana's Sweets."*

Anastasia pulled out her phone and took a picture before calling Ariana. "Ari!" she gushed when her call was answered. "The sign, it's absolutely marvelous!"

Ariana chuckled. "Glad you like it, Ana. I hate to leave, but I have a gyno appointment in like… now. So I'll talk to you later. Meet at Lights?"

"Can we meet at Poison instead?" Anastasia secretly wanted to see if Christopher was there, for there still hadn't been any word from him. She was sure he had liked her, hadn't he?

"Sure, see you later!"

Anastasia decided that she would need to make flyers, and she had excellent photo manipulation skills. So she walked towards her apartment, reassuring herself that it was alright that Christopher hadn't called and that he would soon.

Love for Dessert

The hours passed by quickly, and as the clock hit eight, Anastasia had finished and printed out an abundance of copies to be put up around town. There was a text waiting from Ariana, letting Anastasia know that she was already there and to dress a little more risqué, for they were going to party hard tonight. Ariana was getting a little wilder these days, as she knew that once she was married, she had to tone herself down and be a good wife. Anastasia chuckled as she grabbed a sexy red dress from her closet, obliging Ariana's wishes. She put on more makeup than usual and picked a bright red lipstick to match her dress.

Black heels added inches to her height and her black designer bag swung by her side. She felt confident, and beautiful as she flagged down a taxi. She arrived at Poison a few minutes later, and looked around the front, searching for Ariana.

"Ana!" she heard as she turned her head and saw her best friend running in her platform heels, dressed in an equally scandalous little black dress. "Alright, so we drink a little here, then we go party at this club, where I know the bouncer. He can get us through without waiting in line." Ariana had her hand on the door and was about to push when Anastasia stopped. She had spotted someone familiar, walking down the street with a woman on his arm. Christopher. "Do you know him?" Ariana asked as she checked him out. "He's hot."

"I… We slept together a couple days ago when I was drunk. I left my number for him but… he never called. I guess he wasn't interested." Anastasia watched as the couple stopped walking and kissed passionately. She felt rather crushed that it was just a one-night stand, but there was nothing she could do about it. "I really thought we had a connection though…"

"Do you want to go directly to the club? It kinda looks like they're coming towards this bar." Ariana was concerned about Anastasia, and didn't want her to be upset. This was supposed to be a fun night, and she didn't want whoever this guy was to ruin it.

"Yeah, let's get out of here." Ariana hooked her arm through Anastasia's and they headed off to the nightclub.

"Forget about that loser. There are plenty of available men at this club. Hey, Jonas," Ariana said to the dark-skinned, extremely muscled bouncer at the front. "I'm friends with Nat." The bouncer nodded and let them inside.

And Ariana was right. The club was one of the newer ones, and was packed. It had loud pulsing music that made the walls shake, and Anastasia could feel excitement coursing through her. Ariana was right, there were many attractive men tonight.

Love for Dessert

Anastasia and Ariana headed to the bar first. "Try a new drink tonight. Be spontaneous!" Ariana winked.

"Alright, alright. I'll have... the Manhattan."

Ariana grinned. "Good girl. And I'll have a Bloody Mary, please."

They got their drinks quickly, with Ariana downing about half of hers in one go. "Damn, girl, slow down!" Anastasia gave her a look of amusement. "You're going to get alcohol poisoning."

"Aw, don't worry about me, chill out!" Ariana giggled and slightly hiccupped as she grabbed Anastasia's hand and pulled her out to the dance floor. "Let's dance!"

Anastasia smiled as she began to move her body, showing off her great figure. A man sidled up to her, and began grinding behind her. She whirled around, and found herself face to face with a burly Filipino man, who stared creepily at her through his beady little eyes. She winced as she smiled awkwardly and moved away from him. She found herself near the wall, a somewhat secluded place since everyone else was dancing on the floor.

She stood there, watching Ariana have the time of her life. She looked so happy, and Anastasia was glad that her best friend was so delighted.

"Dragged here against your will, too?" came a voice to her left, and she turned to see an oddly dressed, rather attractive man. He looked young, and his sweater was a contrast to the wifebeaters and tank tops that the other men wore.

She laughed. "My best friend felt like having some fun." Anastasia pointed a finger at Ariana, who was whooping and shaking her hips like there was no tomorrow.

He laughed. "Mine is out there somewhere too, probably hitting on chicks that he'll never get." He had a nice smile, and though he didn't look incredibly sexy, he looked wholesome and very out of place at this nightclub. "Hi, I'm Daniel." He stretched out a hand.

"Anastasia." She shook his hand, blushing slightly.

"You look too beautiful to be standing here chatting with silly old me…" Daniel grinned boyishly, showing off his adorable dimples.

"Aw, thank you." She blushed, suddenly feeling slightly self-conscious under his gaze.

"So what is it you do?" he questioned, wanting to find out more about her.

And for the rest of the evening, Anastasia didn't party hard, nor did she get drunk, but she did get to know Daniel Fields, someone who she found nice and attractive. Though Ariana did eventually drag her out to the dance floor, Anastasia managed to give him her number, and unlike Christopher, he promised to call.

"It's one in the morning, Ari, don't you think we should call it a night?" Anastasia shouted over the loud music. "My feet are killing me!" She didn't look, but she bet she had gigantic blisters on her heels. It certainly felt that way.

"Fine, fine!" Ariana groaned. "Let's go. I may have drunk a little too much…" She chuckled loudly as Anastasia pulled her off the dance floor.

"I'll hail a taxi." As soon as Anastasia and Ariana hit the cold outside air, Ariana's stomach lurched.

She leaned onto Anastasia with wobbling feet. "Ana, I don't feel so good…"

Anastasia sighed. "Alright, let's get you home to Peter… He'll know what to do." Ariana mumbled in consent as they climbed into the yellow taxi.

They reached Ariana's apartment quickly as the traffic was light at one a.m. Anastasia had already texted Peter, letting him know they were on their way. He met them at the bottom of their apartment building, and took Ariana off her hands. "Thanks, Ana. You're a saint."

"No problem and I'd love to stay and chat but it looks like Ariana's about to throw up. You might want to get her to a garbage can."

Love for Dessert

Peter nodded and thanked Anastasia again before carrying Ariana inside. Anastasia climbed back into the taxi and headed home. She felt her phone vibrate, and pulled it out, finding a text waiting for her from an unknown number. *Hey, Anastasia, this is Daniel. Remember me? Haha. I really enjoyed talking to you tonight, and I was wondering if you wanted to grab a cup of coffee or something. Perhaps tomorrow?* She smiled as she entered his number into her contacts.

She was thinking of what to reply with when another text came. *I hope texting you like this isn't too early. I know some guys say to wait a couple days, but I really like you. I mean. Yeah. Sorry.* Anastasia chuckled, for he was being so cute about the whole affair. It was obvious that this wasn't his strong suit.

She texted back quickly. *Tomorrow sounds great, how about noon?* And just like that, she had another date. Anastasia smiled to herself all the way home, excited that here was a man who was interested in her, and wanted to take her out on a real, proper date.

Tomorrow was going to be a big day, not only did she have a date but she had to put up all the flyers. Anastasia collapsed onto the bed as she drifted off to sleep, dreaming of the wonderful life that was coming.

Love for Dessert

***

Anastasia picked out a nice shirt and black trousers for her date. Her hair was freshly washed, her makeup neatly applied and her nail polish reapplied. She was excited for her date, and had brought all the flyers with her in her bag. She headed to the coffee shop, where she was meeting Daniel.

He was already there waiting for her, and was holding two drinks. He was wearing a clean brown sweater, and looked very handsome. "Hi." His face lit up as he spotted her walking towards him. "You look wonderful." He handed her a cup of something hot. "I-I don't really know what you like, but this is a vanilla latte."

"Oh, thank you, Daniel. You're so sweet." She smiled warmly as he pulled out her chair for her, and she sat down gratefully. It had been a while since someone had done something like that for her, and it was nice to know that he really cared. Daniel had that look in his eyes that showed Anastasia that he really did like her, and genuinely wanted to be here with her. He was completely attentive and was interested in everything she said.

Not once did their conversation dull and stop.

As they talked, Anastasia found herself enjoying his company, but for some reason, she didn't find herself completely attracted to him. She brushed it off as nothing, for it was probably just some emotional block she had put up or something. There was no reason to not find Daniel attractive, with his classic boyish looks and his relaxed personality.

They both left the coffeehouse happy, with hope for future dates. But Anastasia's thoughts couldn't linger on Daniel for too long, she had to put up those flyers. They were adorable ones, personally designed by Ariana. They were in the shape of cupcakes, and other various desserts. Anastasia had it all planned out. On their opening day, they would have free drinks, and lowered prices on all the goodies that she would be baking. Unfortunately, she didn't have enough money in the budget to hire an extra hand, though it would truly be helpful. Ariana had offered to help, which was a godsend.

As the sun began to set, all the flyers had been put up. It had been a long day's work, and Anastasia felt like she had walked a million miles. Anastasia smiled as she surveyed her work, standing at the end of a long road, staring at the multicolored pieces of paper firmly tacked to various objects. The final thing she had to do was to go home and research new recipes for the contest.

All too soon, as Anastasia hurried around her apartment's kitchen, trying out new desserts, it was midnight. She still had not found the perfect recipe, and was running out of things to try. She had taste tested so many things that she felt incredibly bloated. Sighing, Anastasia piled all the dishes into the sink, to be cleaned later. She fell asleep soon after, dreaming of sugar cookies and cheesecakes.

***

Anastasia was woken up in the morning by the sound of her ringtone and the powerful vibration of her phone. She checked the caller ID, and smiled when she saw it was Daniel. "Hello?" she answered sleepily.

"Good morning, Anastasia. I hope I didn't wake you up!"

She rubbed her eyes as she sat up, stretching her arms out wide. "Ah, it's nothing, don't worry… What's going on?" Anastasia ran a hand through her long flowing hair.

"Oh, nothing much, I just had a fantastic time the other day and I was wondering if you'd like to have dinner tonight. I hope you're not sick of me already." He laughed.

"I'd be delighted to have dinner. What did you have in mind?" She got out of bed and headed to the kitchen to get herself a glass of water to drink.

Daniel made an "mmm'" sound as he thought. "I was thinking my place, at seven? I'm a hell of a chef, if I do say so myself." He sounded rather proud of himself.

Love for Dessert

"Alright, sounds good." She gave him her address, and he promised to be there on time to pick her up. She liked a man who was punctual.

"So what've you got planned for the rest of the day?" he asked, genuinely interested in her.

Anastasia was just about to answer when her other line rang. It was her mother. "Oh, damn, hey, I'll have to talk to you later, it's my mother on the other line." Daniel said he understood and that he would see her soon, at seven. "Hey, Mom," Anastasia answered as Erica's loud voice filled her ear.

"Anastasia! How's that search for a husband going? I have good news!" Erica didn't give Anastasia any time to reply back. "I'm getting married!" Anastasia sighed and didn't say anything; she knew that Erica would continue speaking on her own. "To George! Isn't he just a total sweetheart?"

"I wouldn't know, Mom. I haven't met him yet." Anastasia rolled her eyes.

"Not to worry, darling, you'll meet him very, very soon. How about tonight?" Erica was always making last-minute plans, and she always assumed Anastasia had a free schedule.

Anastasia was suddenly more grateful than ever for Daniel. She had an excuse not to spend the evening with her mom. She was very glad that her mother had a man in her life to keep her distracted.

Love for Dessert

"Sorry, Mom, I'm busy tonight."

Erica tut-tutted in a disapproving manner. "What do you have to do that could *possibly* be more important than your own mother?"

Anastasia knew that there was no point in lying. "I have a date." Her mother made such a noise from the excitement that Anastasia had to pull the phone away from her ear in order not to go deaf. "Mom, is that really needed?!"

"Oh, I'm just so excited for you!" Erica answered, completely ignoring Anastasia's question. "Can I meet him? What's his name? Is he cute? Is he better looking than he-who-must-not-be-named?"

"Why don't you just ask me when we're getting married?" Anastasia responded sarcastically. "His name is Daniel and he's a nice man, who likes me and I like him."

"That's lovely, honey. Alright, fine, I'll let you off this *one* time. You have a good time with…" She paused and giggled a little. "Daniel."

"Mooom. Are you sixteen?" Anastasia said as she laughed. "Anyway, I'll talk to you later, for sure. I'll call you back later. Love you!" She made a kissing noise before hanging up.

She collapsed onto the bed as she felt her phone vibrate. It was another sweet text from Daniel, letting her know that he was thinking about her, and couldn't wait to see her tonight. Anastasia blushed as she felt delighted to have a man who adored her this much. He certainly was a catch, and she felt lucky to have caught him.

There was an email waiting for Anastasia in her inbox from the baking contest coordinators. It informed her of the venue, a quaint park, and how the contestants were to make the goods. They were to meet at two in the afternoon, and all the utensils, ovens, and basic ingredients would be prepared. All they had to bring were any special ingredients they needed. There would be a news station covering the entire event. It was a yearly tradition after all, and was a big deal.

Anastasia had lots of time to kill before her date, and she was determined to find the perfect recipe. She had already decided on making a sweet dish, but nothing she currently knew tasted or looked correct. It had to be perfect, for winning this contest could bring her a lot of success. She really needed the cash reward and having a news story done would definitely bring more customers in. Anastasia sighed as her fingers flew across her laptop's keyboard, searching for the perfect dessert.

Half an hour later, Anastasia still couldn't find a cake that fit exactly what she was looking for. She sighed as she sat back in her chair and stared up at the ceiling, wracking her brain for some obscure recipe she might have tucked into the very corners of her mind. She came up empty. But then, just as she was about to give up, inspiration struck. She could mix two recipes together, and create something new entirely!

Anastasia knew her best two cakes were the angel food cake, and the devil's food cake. The last time she had made them, Ariana had eaten half of both even though she had been on a diet. If she layered the cakes and put a thick layer of icing in between… Oh, it would be delicious. Her mouth watered just thinking about it. She couldn't wait any longer. Anastasia leapt up from her seat and into the shower as she prepared to go to the grocery store to pick up the necessary ingredients.

Anastasia was out on the town in half an hour, ready to go. She had texted Ariana, letting her know that she was baking Ariana's favorite tonight. Ariana texted back with six happy faces, obviously extremely excited. As Anastasia surveyed the vegetable aisle, she noticed a man at the end checking her out. She grinned as she watched him take in her long, tanned legs that were shown off by her tight shorts and her nice ample chest. Ever since she had quit her job, she didn't have to be confined by the office dressing rules.

As soon as Anastasia got back to her apartment, she began to bake, mixing all sorts of things together and

Love for Dessert

creating amazing smells. "God damn, that smells good!" she exclaimed as she dipped a finger into the light colored batter, tasting the sweetness. "Yum." She smiled as she stuck the pan into her oven. She was in a fantastic mood, having just found the recipe of her dreams. She would win, for sure.

A knock came at the door and Anastasia opened it gleefully. Ariana stood in the doorway with Peter, their hands entwined lovingly. "Hey, girl, I'm here for the taste testing! And I hope you don't mind, I brought the fiancé." They both smiled brightly. Peter Gold was an older-looking man, though he was only twenty-seven. He wasn't incredibly attractive, though Ariana had always found there was a certain kind of charm about him.

Peter ran a hand through his jet-black hair. "Thanks for inviting us, Ana." He was always very polite, even though they knew each other so well. "Ari tells me that you're quite the excellent baker, but you're very shy about it." He winked at her as they both stepped into the apartment.

This was the first time Peter had been to the apartment since Aaron left, and it looked so different. It would be rude of him to point it out, but he could see how deeply Aaron had affected her. Anastasia happily took out half of the finished cake, beautifully placed on an intricately decorated silver cake plate.

Love for Dessert

"Damn, Ana, that looks amazing." Ariana's eyes gleamed as she stared at the cake. The layers were deliberately stacked in a pattern of dark and light. "What's this cake called?" she said as she cut herself a thick slice. "And what the heck is it made of?"

"You took such a big slice without knowing what it is?" Peter laughed.

Anastasia explained. "It's made of a devil's food cake stacked onto an angel food cake, and then stacked again. And it's all stuck together with chocolate and vanilla icing. I haven't really thought of a name yet though. Just try it, let me know what you think."

Ariana grinned. "Don't mind if I do!" She stuck a fork into it and took a bite. Anastasia watched as her eyes lit up. "Delicious!" She fed a bite to Peter, who had an equally good response.

"If you make this for those judges, they're really going to be impressed!" He grinned. "Also, since it's made of angel food cake and devil's food cake, perhaps you should call it Heaven and Hell?"

"That's a fantastic idea, Peter, thanks so much." Anastasia felt proud to have created her own cake, and that now it had a name. It certainly was unique, and looked good, too.

"So what're you doing tonight? Peter and I were going to see a movie, you could come along if you'd like," Ariana offered.

Love for Dessert

"As much as I'd love to come be a third wheel, I actually have a date tonight. He's coming to pick me up at seven."

"He!? Who is he? That boy I saw you talking to at the club? He's adorable! And he didn't look too wild. What's his name? I want details!" Ariana reminded Anastasia of Erica, in a good way.

"He's called Daniel, and he's pretty cute if I do say so myself." Anastasia smiled.

Ariana checked her watch. "It's almost six, have you picked out what to wear yet?" she asked.

"Ari, honey, maybe we should leave, and give Anastasia time to prepare for her date," Peter said wisely as he watched his fiancée polish off her slice of cake.

"Fine, fine," Ariana grumbled. "Can I take some of the cake to go? Please?"

Anastasia nodded as she took out a Tupperware container. "Here you go. Have a good time at the movies!" She gave Ariana and Peter one last hug before closing the door and turned her attention onto finding something to wear.

An hour later, five minutes before the clock struck seven, Anastasia stood in front of her full-length mirror, checking herself one last time before Daniel came. She had chosen a flirty black dress and with it she matched red suede high heels. An expensive

Love for Dessert

designer bag hung at her side and silver bangles jangled on her wrist.

There was another knock at the door, just as Anastasia reapplied her dark crimson lipstick. "Coming!" she called out as she walked over to the door. She pulled it open, and saw a smartly dressed Daniel, waiting for her.

"Good evening, beautiful." His lips curved into a smile as he leaned in and gently kissed her on the cheek. "Ready to go?"

"Oh, yes, definitely." Anastasia felt like she couldn't stop smiling as she walked out of her apartment and locked the door behind her. Daniel wrapped a protective arm around her thin waist as they headed down the hallway. He made her laugh uncontrollably as they made their way down to his car.

Daniel's apartment was fantastically furnished, and it was obvious that he had a knack for decorating. All the lights were dimmed romantically, and Daniel led her to the dining room, where she was pleasantly surprised by a candlelit dinner. Daniel pressed a button, and the soothing voice of Michael Bublé started.

"This is amazing, Daniel," she murmured as he pulled out the chair for her and she sat down. "Did you do all of this by yourself? For little old me?" She grinned.

Love for Dessert

"Of course. You're worth it." He sat down across from her, and put his hand on hers.

She looked down at her plate, where a dinner had already been arranged artfully. A steak, cooked to perfection, mashed potatoes, creamy with bits of corn, a delicious gravy dribbled over all the food… A glass of wine stood beside the plate, and she took it in her hands. She watched as he did the same.

"Here's to a wonderful evening." He raised his glass and clinked it against hers.

And a wonderful evening it was.

After she finished her plate, Daniel stood up. "Want to dance?" He took her in his arms and they swayed to the music. He was a perfect gentleman and Anastasia could see herself having a future with him. But unfortunately, as Daniel leaned in to kiss her, she didn't feel it. There was no spark, no passion. He was perfect, but just not for her.

As his lips touched hers, she felt like there was nothing. Even though he didn't use too much tongue, nor did he slobber over her, something was still missing. She pulled away in a couple moments, and he gave her a look of concern.

"Is something wrong?" His voice was soft, and he was genuinely worried about the evening going wrong. Oh, he was so caring and it was breaking her heart.

Love for Dessert

"Daniel..." She pulled out of his arms. "Everything is perfect, but that's the problem. I don't feel anything between us. There's no rush, no passion... You're a wonderful man, Daniel. It's not your fault. It's mine." She hated being so cliché, but there was nothing else that would describe how she felt. She truly liked him, but she would never grow to be in love with him.

But he looked crushed. The look in his eyes made her want to take back everything she had just said but there was no chance of that happening. "I..." he mumbled in a quiet voice. "I understand." She could see how hard he was trying to stay strong and she respected him for it. He was a genuine man, and she knew how much rejection hurt.

She picked up her purse, which had been lying on the sofa in front of them. "I'm sorry, Daniel," she murmured as she headed out the door, not looking back once.

When Anastasia finally reached her apartment, it was late. She collapsed onto her sofa and curled up into a ball as she felt her phone vibrate again. "Who could that be?" Ariana and Peter were probably still at the movies, and Erica was busy with George. It was from Daniel. *I'm sorry for overreacting, Anastasia. You're a wonderful woman, and I hope that we can be friends.*

Anastasia pressed her lips together as she chose not to answer for now. She poured herself a glass of wine,

Love for Dessert

and eventually fell asleep on the couch, dreaming of her bakery.

***

The weeks sped by and pretty soon, it was the day before the baking contest. Anastasia felt completely prepared, and everyone that tried her cake had told her it was delicious. She was confident that she would at least win a secondary prize, if not first. She was excited to meet her competition and was sure that she would learn from them.

The opening day of the bakery drew near. It was set for a couple days after the contest had been completely wrapped up. It was mostly ready, and everything had gone smoothly, save for a little disagreement between Ariana and one of the painters about color. Anastasia was putting the finishing touches on the menu, adding little personal touches here and there.

She had finally texted Daniel back a couple days later, letting him know that she was open to the idea of remaining on friendly terms. He wasn't a bad guy, it was just the fact that there was no chemistry between them. Anastasia smiled as he texted her back something clever. She was having dinner with her mother that night, to meet George, Erica's fiancé. Anastasia picked out a simple blue dress that brought out her eyes, and applied gentle makeup.

Love for Dessert

Her phone rang. It was Erica. "Hi, Mom."

"Honey, are you heading to the restaurant now? George and I are already here." Erica paused, then said in a quieter tone, "George, not now, I'm on the phone with Ana!" She giggled.

Anastasia winced. "Mom, I don't need to hear this stuff, okay? I'll be there soon."

"Uh-huh, okay, sweetie. See you!" Erica laughed before hanging up.

Anastasia rolled her eyes. Erica was so crazy and always acted half her age. She headed out the door and headed towards the restaurant, not wanting to give her mother another excuse to call her again.

Anastasia's first impression of George was exactly what she had expected. He was an older gentleman, yes, but he was still rather handsome. His jaw was chiseled, his eyes sharp. He wore an expensive Rolex on his left wrist. Oh, he was just her mother's usual type. "Hello, I'm Anastasia." She smiled warmly as she shook George's hand.

"Good evening, Anastasia. I'm George." He returned her smile with an equally bright one. Erica watched this happily.

"Sit down, Ana. We already ordered some appetizers. Hope you like calamari."

Love for Dessert

Erica's eyes never left George the entire night. Anastasia could tell how much she really loved him and judging by the size of the rock on her ring finger, he felt the same way towards her. She found herself actually enjoying George's company. He had traveled far and wide, and had many stories to tell about the whole experience.

She learned that he had been married many times, too. And when Erica left the table to go "powder her nose," George had confided in Anastasia that he really felt like her mother was the one. Anastasia had happily given him her blessing.

All of a sudden it seemed like everyone around her was getting married, and Anastasia was the only one being left in the dust. To be completely honest, she was a little scared that she would never find another man that she would feel as much love for as she had for Aaron. But she kept her hopes up.

"Well, Mother, it's getting rather late and I do have that contest to attend tomorrow. I should be heading out." Anastasia swung her bag over her shoulder. "It was really nice to meet you, George." She gave her mother a hug and George a handshake.

"Alright, honey, knock them dead tomorrow! I'm so proud of you." Erica smiled as she linked arms with George again.

Love for Dessert

"Thanks, Mom." Anastasia grinned. "Goodnight!" She headed out of the restaurant and towards her apartment, determined to get a good night's rest before the big contest. She needed to win, for the sake of her bakery, and herself.

***

Anastasia awoke the next morning full of energy. She was eager and looking forward to the competition. She was confident. Anastasia picked out a simple black top, and stylish tribal-patterned joggers. It was all about the comfort today. It was eleven o'clock, and the contest started at twelve thirty. So she hurried to the biggest park in the city, where the contest was to be held, her hands tingling with excitement.

The park was already abuzz with activity, as camera operators and reporters hurried around the park, interviewing citizens. The contest organizers had already set up the ovens and such. Anastasia moved towards the person she assumed was the head coordinator. "Hi, are you a competitor?" He shook her hand warmly. "I'm Eddie."

"Hi, Eddie, yes, I'm Anastasia! From Ana's Sweets."

"Oh, yes, the start-up bakery right? Please, come right over here, we've prepared aprons for you already. Did you bring the extra ingredients you need?" Eddie asked as they walked to one counter/oven setup. There were three other ones that Anastasia assumed were for the other contestants.

Two of the other bakers arrived shortly after, and they looked very experienced. Anastasia set down her items as she surveyed the rest of her competition. One of them, a woman, had short red hair, and a rather stumpy looking appearance. She looked like an older woman, and Anastasia guessed her to be around fifty. Her strong features made her look rather Russian.

Anastasia also noticed that all of the stations had individual names posted on the front. Hers was listed as Anastasia – Ana's Sweets. She leaned over and subtly checked out the red-haired lady. Natalya – Russian Treats, was what it read. Natalya… That was a pretty name. The other competitor's name was Jack, from CORN, a chain bakery.

The last competitor still hadn't arrived. For some reason his bakery's name wasn't printed on his kitchen space, only his first name, Darren. That name was somewhat familiar to her, but she couldn't place it.

Pretty soon, the competition was a half an hour away from starting and Anastasia was nervous. She bit her fingernail as she watched the mysterious Darren take his place behind his baking area. She couldn't get a good look at him, for she was so focused on watching Eddie. But she could tell that Darren was tall.

Love for Dessert

Eddie walked in front of all the contestants. Anastasia noticed that all the cameras were pointed at them, and quite a crowd had gathered. There were seats that had been set out, and all of them were full. Many people were even standing.

"I didn't know this was such a big event..." she mumbled to herself as she began to get more nervous. Everyone else seemed calm, or at least Natalya did. This probably wasn't her first competition. Natalya caught Anastasia looking at her and smiled warmly, like a mother.

Loud, happy music started as Eddie grabbed a microphone and tapped it lightly to make sure it was on. He cleared his throat. "Welcome, everyone, to *So You Think You Can Bake*, the annual baking contest!" He paused, and the audience clapped. "Today, our four talented competitors from various bakeries will be competing for the grand prize of three thousand dollars, plus a news article to be published in the Daily Chronicle. And if that wasn't good enough..." He paused for dramatic effect. "We're also sweetening the deal by adding an extra interview with the local news!"

Anastasia grinned as she caught the eye of Ariana, who was standing with Peter beside a tall tree. Ariana smiled widely and gave Anastasia a thumbs-up.

Eddie began to introduce each contestant, which Anastasia only paid a little attention to until he got to her. "Our third competitor is Anastasia Emmott, who's opening her very own bakery in just a couple of days, called Ana's Sweets! And as her bakery name implies, she's best at making sweet desserts! I'm very excited to see what she makes for our judges today!"

As described by Eddie, the three judges today were renowned chefs. "Be warned, competitors!" Eddie laughed. "They may look friendly, but these judges will be tough on your creation!" He walked to the center of all the mini-kitchens. "Alright, competitors, remember that you have an hour and a half to create your masterpiece. Use your time wisely, there are *no* extensions." He raised his arms up in the air theatrically.

"And now, without further ado... Begin!"

Chapter 3

Anastasia felt a wave of pressure on her. Beads of sweat dripped down her forehead as her brow furrowed in concentration. Everything had to be perfect. She started with the easiest parts, beating the egg, mixing everything together. She had to bake the cakes, arrange them, and finally make it look beautiful. That took a while, and she only had an hour and a half. They had huge clocks on the mini-kitchen counters, letting everyone know how much time they had left.

She knew that it would be a bad idea to rush, but she felt like she would have no choice. She glanced over at Natalya, who was whisking and twirling away, in a world of her own. The confidence she had felt that morning was slowly slipping away as she felt like she was messing everything up, though she had made cakes so many times before. It was surreal, how all the camera lights, the constant murmuring of the crowd, the loud music and whatnot made it many times harder to work.

"I can do this…" she murmured to herself. Within twenty minutes, she had made the batter for both cakes, mixed to perfection. She was beginning to calm down by now, and one of her favorite songs came on. Anastasia began to sing quietly, getting into the groove. Pretty soon, as the song hit the chorus, Anastasia started to move her body, grooving to the music. She forgot all about the audience watching her.

Soon, the cakes were in the oven, baking beautifully. Before long, delicious aromas began to emit from several of the ovens. Anastasia had to wait for ten minutes longer, and she relaxed as she mixed the icing. She turned to watch the other competitors, to see what they were making. Natalya seemed to be making some sort of pudding.

Jack was forming little shapes out of fondant, which was used for the little decorations on top of cupcakes and such. He was probably making those. She could barely see Darren's counter, but he wasn't doing anything either and was simply waiting for his creation to finish baking, she assumed. He turned his head suddenly, and caught her eye. She blushed as she saw his face for the first time.

Oh lord, was he handsome. His chiseled jaw was strong, yet his eyes were so friendly. As he noticed her watching him, he winked and smiled. She swore she could feel her heart melt. He was wearing a tank top, showing off his strong, muscled arms. It was obvious that he worked out regularly. His eyes were so dark, she couldn't place the exact color. His hair was cut in a very natural way that she liked. He didn't look like a baker, but obviously he had to be somewhat good to be selected for the competition.

Love for Dessert

All of a sudden, Anastasia felt her heart beat faster and her breathing became slightly more agitated as she returned his smile. He held her gaze for a moment longer before turning back to his goods, which were probably done baking. Anastasia kept watching him, in a way that she hoped was subtle. Anastasia thought about his strong sinewy arms wrapped around her, keeping her secure and making her feel very, *very* safe.

Ding! Anastasia was snapped out of her fantasy by the sound of her oven going off. Oh, her third layer of cake was ready! She happily opened the door to the oven and was greeted by black smoke. "Crap, crap, crap! There's smoke!" Anastasia went into panic mode as she pulled out the tray of devil's food cake and discovered that it was completely burnt. "How?!" she exclaimed.

"Damn it!" Anastasia yelled. There was only fifty minutes left on the clock, and she only had the first two alternating layers ready. "Okay, breathe, Ana, you have to breathe and calm down. Just make another batch. It'll be easy," she murmured as she began to quickly mix the ingredients. She only had enough special ingredients left to make one more tray of the cake. This was her last chance to make things perfect.

It would be tight, and tough to make it on time, but she was determined to do it.

Love for Dessert

As she waited, Anastasia began to hurriedly spread the chocolate icing onto the first layer of cake. She could still win, it was just harder. She dumped the angel food cake out as the crowd oohed. "Now, all the contestants only have forty-five minutes left!" Eddie announced. "I hope they're all ready for presenting soon. Mmm! It all smells so delicious! Hope it tastes as good as it smells!" He laughed gleefully.

Anastasia soon had the first two layers done and ready to go. She still had to make two more layers in addition to the one that was still baking. Thankfully she had already made those batters, and only had to stick them in the oven. She breathed, "I can do this." Anastasia grinned happily as she pulled out the third layer, and put in the fourth. She was working like a well-oiled machine, and though she longed to look over and stare at Darren forever, she knew that she had to concentrate.

The clock continued to tick on, and pretty soon, there was only fifteen minutes left. Inspiration had hit Anastasia as she saw a jar of peanut butter sitting on the counter, and she had used that mixed with some other ingredients as the filling instead of the icing in between the cakes. She hoped it would add a unique flavor.

Finally, just as the countdown clock hit ten minutes, she had iced almost all of the cake. She just had the top to decorate, and some chocolate shavings to add. She had done an excellent job, and it was clear to the audience that she had skill. Anastasia added a splotch of melted white chocolate onto the cake, and using a toothpick, made a chevron pattern on the top. She grabbed a handful of the chocolate pieces, and artistically arranged them.

"Oh, damn, Anastasia's cake sure looks good!" Eddie exclaimed as he shot her a smile and watched her inspect her creation. Natalya's pudding turned out to be multilayered, and looked incredibly complex and rather traditional.

All too soon, the clocks ticked down to zero and an incredibly obnoxious buzzer rung. "Alright, contestants, time is up! Please step away from your kitchen. Our wonderful servers will bring your creations to the judging table." As he spoke, girls in waitress outfits walked onto the makeshift stage and grabbed the masterpieces, which had been placed on beautiful dessert dishes.

Eddie directed all the contestants to the front of the stage, and everyone turned their heads to watch the judges taste. One of the judges made a little gasp of delight upon cutting open Anastasia's cake, revealing the wonderfully crafted layers inside. They didn't take too long to taste the delicious samples. "Alright, let's hear some comments from our judges!"

Love for Dessert

The first judge, an older man who didn't really smile, picked up his microphone. "Well, starting with Anastasia's delightful 'Heaven and Hell' cake…" The judges had nothing but compliments for her. They really loved the peanut butter idea, and thought the layering was a unique twist on the recipe.

They didn't praise Jack's cupcakes as much, saying that they were somewhat dry, though the toppings, which consisted of tiny little roses with green leaves, were incredibly cute. Natalya's pudding was sweet and crunchy, and Anastasia had guessed correctly, it was a traditional Russian dish. And last but not least, they reached Darren's bread, which looked like a normal garlic toast. But as they cut it open, the judges were delighted to find that there was melted cheese inside, throwing a different taste into the mix.

"Well, while the judges are deliberating, we'll let the contestants mingle. It won't take too long! And as for the audience, take your guesses as to be who the winner will be!" The minutes ticked by slowly as Anastasia chatted with Natalya. But she noticed that Darren kept watching her. She longed to do the same, but it wouldn't do her any good to be too obvious.

"Alright, we're back, and our wonderful judges have made a decision!" All the contestants lined up. Anastasia's hands shook slightly in excitement. Oh, lord, she really hoped she was the winner. "Let's hear it from the judge herself!"

Love for Dessert

The female judge in the middle stood up. "Yes, Eddie, thanks. It was hard, but we finally decided. Staring with a very close second place... With a delicious and unique baked good... A big congratulations to Mister Darren King!" The loud applause was deafening as Darren stepped up to claim his prize, a check for the amount of five hundred dollars.

Anastasia crossed her fingers behind her back as she blinked nervously. This was the moment. It was all or nothing.

"And in first place..." The judge obviously had a flair for the dramatic. "Anastasia Emmott! According to the judges, your unique cake was delicious, appealing to the eyes, and completely amazing." Anastasia's eyes flew open in surprise.

"I won! I really won!" she yelled as she stared at Ariana with happiness in her eyes.

Ariana smiled crazily as she jumped up and down, clapping her hands, mouthing "yay." This was an amazing moment, and Anastasia felt like she would never be unhappy again. It was such an amazing opportunity for her and her bakery, and everything was starting off perfectly. Life was looking up. She was starting a new chapter of her life, and she couldn't be happier.

Love for Dessert

Eddie pulled out a comically large check that had "three thousand dollars" written on it. Anastasia couldn't speak, she was so stunned and excited. She walked towards Eddie as he handed her the check. They posed, and smiled widely for the camera. "A very big congratulations to Miss Anastasia Emmott! Please, step right over here, where you will be interviewed by the news crew."

The loud music started up again as Anastasia followed Eddie off the stage and did her interview. Ariana and Peter waited in the wings for her to finish. After the live interview, the reporters from the newspaper came and talked to her. By the time they finished, it was already getting late, and was nearing dinner time.

"Hey, Ana, girl, I am so proud of you!" Ariana squeezed her friend tightly in an embarrassing hug. "Let's go celebrate. Food!" She grinned as Peter wrapped an arm around her. It was a simple gesture, one Anastasia saw all the time, but all of a sudden it hit her with a pang that she was still alone. Though she was so happy about winning, and felt that it was truly a blessing, she couldn't help but feel that something was missing. Ariana continued to speak. "Okay, so…" She paused.

Ariana and Peter smiled coyly as they stopped talking and stepped back a little. "What's wrong?" Anastasia stepped back and bumped into something. She whirled around, and came face to face with the tall, handsome Darren. "Oh!" She emitted a little yelp as she leapt back. She heard laughter coming from Ariana and Peter behind her.

"Hi," he said in a deep, husky voice that sent chills down her spine.

"A-ah, hello." She was startled, but pleasantly surprised that it was Darren she had bumped into. He was even more attractive up close, if that was even possible. He *really* didn't look like a baker! And she liked it.

"Sorry for startling you…" He crossed his arms, showing off his muscles. She had to focus her eyes on his face, determined not to stare at his muscles, however attractive they were. "I was just coming over to congratulate you on first place."

Anastasia blushed prettily. "Oh, thank you! Congratulations yourself, on second place! Your bread looked very delicious, it's a shame that I couldn't have a taste." He smiled at her compliment.

"Well, I could always make it for you myself sometime." Anastasia could hardly think straight. Was this gorgeous man offering to cook for her himself? Possibly on a date? "That is, if you want." But she did remember Christopher, and how he had charmed her. He too was a good-looking man, and she didn't want to walk the same path again.

Love for Dessert

"Oh, that sounds lovely." She tucked a stray strand of hair behind her ear and licked her upper lip, something she only did when she was trying to look nice.

"How about tonight? My place? I promise you, no evil intentions." He grinned genuinely and for some reason, she found herself believing him completely.

But she was already going out with Ariana and Peter tonight. Or so she thought. She turned back to look at her friends. "Uh…" Before she even spoke, Ariana knew what she was going to say.

"Go!" Ariana grinned.

Anastasia laughed. Ariana already knew what she was thinking before she said it. She truly was her best friend. "Thanks, Ari."

Ariana stood beside Peter as she watched Anastasia and Darren talk, as proud as a mother at graduation. Darren was a catch, and she and Anastasia both knew it. "I guess I'm free now for the night!" She grinned happily.

"Great. You can drop by my place, say around seven?" He gave her his address. "Don't eat before then, I'll be preparing a feast," he joked and shot her another wink. Oh, she would be content just staring at his face for the entire night, for he was so incredibly good-looking.

Love for Dessert

"It's a date!" She laughed as she twirled a piece of her blond hair within her fingers, making her look very cute and young.

"It certainly is. I have to go now, but I'll see you later tonight?" Darren kept smiling, and she felt rather shy.

"For sure."

He winked once more before turning away. Anastasia gleefully turned around and smiled brightly at Ariana. "Oh my God! He asked me over to his place for a home-cooked dinner!"

"Wow, the boy moves fast." Ariana laughed. "But he is *so* good-looking!" she gushed.

Peter shot her an amused look. "Too bad you're engaged," he said as he grabbed her hand and entwined their fingers.

"Yes, too bad. But Anastasia isn't!" The three began to walk towards the exit of the park, chattering away. "So, what're you going to wear tonight?"

***

Anastasia was home a little while later, still bubbling with excitement. She had to pick out the perfect thing. She turned on her television to the news, and was greeted by her own face. There was a reporter speaking, one that had interviewed her earlier. "Earlier this evening, the annual *So You Think You Can Bake* was held in the park. The second place

Love for Dessert

winner, Darren King, made an excellent cheese bread. And the grand prize winner, seen with me here, Anastasia Emmott, made an incredible Heaven and Hell cake. So Anastasia, why did you enter the contest?"

She laughed as she watched herself speak on television. She looked so nervous, yet happy. "I entered to try to win some more funding for and also to promote my new bakery, which is opening tomorrow. It's called Ana's Sweets, and we'll be serving many different kinds of desserts, like cupcakes, brownies and cakes. Please swing by if you can to our grand opening, tomorrow at nine thirty. We'll be giving out samples of all our baked goods. And you can even try the Heaven and Hell cake that I made here today."

Anastasia smiled as she saw how well the interview went. She kept it on in the background as she selected a simple black dress. "Hmm…" She pursed her lips and then decided that tonight she was going to have fun and her dress shouldn't be so boring. She opted instead for a colorful gradient purple dress that showed off her long legs. The low cut of the top revealed a bit of her ample bosom. She had no plans to go far with Darren tonight, but there was no harm in teasing him a bit.

It was six fifteen, and all Anastasia had to do was put on her makeup. She did it quickly, what with her years

Love for Dessert

of practice. She checked in her full-length mirror to make sure she looked good, before heading out and hailing a taxi. Darren lived in a small apartment building, and it was clear to her that he obviously wasn't incredibly rich. But that was fine.

She knocked on the door politely and heard loud shuffling sounds inside. The door swung open and there he stood, in a nice open-neck silk shirt that barely concealed his muscles. There was a twinkling in his eyes of something she couldn't place, but it excited her. There was a delicious smell in the air, and it made her mouth water. "Good evening." His voice was low, and rumbling.

"Hi" was all she could say as she smiled widely, excitement taking over. "That smells really good."

"Ah, ha-ha." He laughed. "Please, come in."

It was an odd apartment. It was obviously decorated by someone with little to no decorating skills whatsoever. There was a black couch with oddly colored green and red pillows. Little knickknacks lay on the coffee table. Several paintings were hung on the walls, of abstract pictures and shapes. There was a small dining table in the corner.

"Sorry, there isn't much in my apartment since I live alone," he said sheepishly as he scratched his head. "Please, take a seat." There were plates set up already. "I'll bring the food out."

Love for Dessert

It turned out that Darren had made a full three-course meal, starting with the cheesy bread he had made as an appetizer. Anastasia ate as politely as she could. "Wow, this is amazing!" she said as she swallowed the cheesy substance, baked to perfection. "I can't believe you didn't win first place. I could eat this forever!"

Darren laughed heartily. "I'm glad you like it. It doesn't matter that I didn't win, I've already got a job at the bakery. You really deserve to win, plus you need the money, right? For your new bakery?"

Anastasia nodded, a light smile on her face. "Yes! Did you watch my interview? I think I looked kind of weird on television."

"You looked beautiful," he said honestly as he dropped his fork and stared into her eyes.

She could feel her cheeks growing hot and red as she returned his gaze. "O-oh..." she murmured. "Thank you." She paused for a moment, trying to regain her composure. "W-would you like to come to the grand opening?"

Darren frowned. "Unfortunately, as much as I would love to, I have work."

"Where do you work?" she asked curiously as she ate.

"At the bakery close to yours, actually," he replied.

Love for Dessert

"Maybe I'll visit you tomorrow, if I can." He laughed awkwardly at her comment. She didn't notice, and continued on happily eating her meal.

The rest of the evening was completely perfect. After dinner, they curled up onto the couch to watch a movie. He even let her pick which one, and she was surprised to find that he had several romantic chick flicks. He even got so bold as to wrap an arm around her shoulder halfway through, and she let him. Soon it was time to say goodbye, for she had to wake up early in the morning to bake. He kissed her on the cheek like a gentleman before letting her go, with promises that he would call her.

Anastasia fell asleep that night with a happy smile on her lips.

***

It was seven o'clock, on the day of the opening. Anastasia rubbed her tired eyes as she worked, not stopping for an instant. She couldn't afford to, after all. Pretty soon there were going to be, she hoped, lots of people at the grand opening. The door jangled as Ariana came in, dragging a tired-looking Peter.

"Hey, we're here to help out. Need me to mix stuff?" Anastasia nodded as she tossed her friends two aprons. They got to work, kneading, mixing, pouring, shaping and rolling. Pretty soon, the bakery was filled with all kinds of delightful smells. The sun was high in the sky by the time they finished baking, and it was nine o'clock, half an hour to opening. A somewhat substantial crowd of people gathered, and Ariana was still busy blowing up balloons.

The half an hour sped by as Anastasia rushed around the shop preparing everything. Her mother had promised to swing by later, to make sure that her money had not gone to waste. Typical. Very soon, it was time to open those doors. Anastasia was wearing comfy white Ked sneakers, with a very cute apron. She was ready to serve.

Peter had already set up small tables, with stylish chairs. Anastasia had long ago decided that her bakery would also be a sort of café, where customers could sit and eat what they had bought. "Are we ready to open, Ana?" Peter asked as he rearranged the tablecloths again. He and Ariana had brought matching aprons, and were ready to serve the hungry customers.

"Just one thing to do before we open." Anastasia skipped gleefully over to the large stereo system, and fiddled with a couple buttons. A couple seconds later she pressed the big black button. Upbeat music filtered out of the several music speakers Anastasia had purchased a couple days ago. "Now we're ready."

She moved to the front doors and took a deep breath before pulling the doors open. "We are officially open for business!"

Love for Dessert

***

Though the day started off with not that many people, as the day dragged on, quite a large crowd made their way into Ana's Sweets. Anastasia rushed around the kitchen like mad, making several different cakes at once, all of her ovens in use. There wasn't a moment to spare as the demand was great. People tasted a sample, liked it, then ordered more. She was making so much.

As she worked, she caught comments that some patrons made on her food.

"This cake is delicious!"

"Wow, this is like heaven in my mouth, definitely not hell!"

"We need to come here more. Loving the drinks!"

Anastasia was glad to hear that last statement for she had just added in the drinks menu that consisted of typical beverages such as lemonade, tea, coffee, and others. Though it was a little odd to have drinks in a bakery, Anastasia thought her customers would appreciate having something to drink so that the baked goods would not dry their throats. She felt lucky that many people truly enjoyed the drinks. Peter was the one making them, for Anastasia had yet to hire an assistant. She couldn't really afford to either, unfortunately.

Love for Dessert

"Seems like customers are really responding to this, Ana." Peter grinned happily as he continued to make drinks.

"I know, I'm so happy!" Anastasia turned back to the cash register. "Hello, how can I help you?" She smiled widely at the two teenage-looking girls waiting at the counter.

"Two slices of the Heaven and Hell cake, please! And I just want to say, you look so pretty in person! I love your apron."

Anastasia blushed as they gushed over her. "Oh, thank you so much." She chuckled as she took their money and handed them their cake. "Thank you! Have a great day."

It certainly was turning out to be a wonderful day, and Anastasia felt truly blessed to have this many people show up, friends and family included, to support her. Everything was going smoothly, and Darren texted her, letting her know that even though he couldn't be there in person to support her, she was still on his mind and he wanted to see her that night. His sweet and thoughtful text put a silly girlish smile on her face. She quickly made arrangements with him to pick her up at eight.

There had been one small hiccup, though. During a short break she took, she headed over to the bakery across the street to visit Darren, but the sweet old man who ran the shop said that Darren wasn't scheduled to work. It was odd that he would lie to her about it, but she pushed it away in her mind as something he had probably just forgotten or remembered mistakenly. No big deal, right?

The hours sped by and soon, it was seven o'clock, which signaled the end of the grand opening day. It had been a long day, and by the time she closed up and hugged Ariana and Peter goodbye, it was already seven thirty. She only had half an hour to get home and get ready for whatever Darren had prepared for them. Unfortunately, as she hailed a taxi, on her way home, Anastasia found herself stuck in a heavy traffic jam.

"Damn it," she muttered as she watched the minutes tick by, getting later and later. It was seven fifty by the time she got home, and she was panicking. She was still in her slightly flour-covered apron and her hair was a mess. She quickly pulled on the first clean things she could find out of her closet, and ended up in a plain white top and light blue jeans. There was no time to change into anything else, only a couple minutes to lightly apply a thin layer of makeup.

Anastasia was only able to put on a bit of eyeliner and mascara before she was stopped by the loud ringing of the doorbell. "Crap, he's here." She headed to the door quickly as she grabbed her wallet and phone along the way. She pulled it open, and there he was. "Hi."

He grinned as he saw her. "Sorry if I'm staring, you look beautiful." She was so happy that he thought her still beautiful even when she wasn't dressed up.

Darren had made reservations for them at a nice restaurant, and they had a wonderful time discussing the bakery, and Anastasia's plans for the future, among other things. Anastasia was captivated by his kind eyes, his caring personality and his attractive body. She could feel her heart beating faster every time she saw him and she felt like she could tell him anything.

Near the end of the night, after they had just finished dessert and were drinking the last of their wine, Darren reached across the table and covered her hand with his. "Anastasia… I don't know if this is moving too fast, or if it seems desperate, but during these past couple days, I've really grown to feel like we are incredibly compatible. You're so beautiful, funny and smart. I haven't met anyone like you before. Would you…" He paused, genuinely shy. "Would you be my girlfriend?"

She was so delighted that she giggled. "Yes, Darren, I will."

Love for Dessert

***

Though it was still early in the morning, Anastasia awoke with a newfound joy in her heart. It was a nice feeling, to be wanted. She was excited to be working in her new bakery, and judging by yesterday's turnout, there would be a lot of people coming. There was a morning text from Darren waiting for her on her phone, which made her smile. *Good morning, girlfriend, hope you had a good sleep. I miss seeing you already.* It was somewhat juvenile and reminded her of high school, but in a good way.

At eight, Anastasia opened her doors, looking forward to another day. It was nice being her own boss. The first couple hours crept by slowly with an average amount of customers. Many of them were friendly and willing to make small talk with her, which she enjoyed. But as soon as the clock hit three, an abundance of students poured in, for school had just ended.

They praised her baked goods loudly and happily, swearing that they would tell all their friends about this delightful little bakery. Anastasia couldn't help but smile as she watched them enjoy what she had created. She was also looking forward to seeing Darren again, so she texted him. *Are you free tonight?*

He texted back quickly. *Can't. Have to help sort out mess at work. The old man who runs the shop… had a heart*

Love for Dessert

attack. He's in the hospital. Might not make it. I'll have to work all the way until closing.

Anastasia gasped in surprise. He had seemed like such a nice man the time she had briefly met him and she hoped that he would pull through. The bell above the door rung as it swung open, letting in another big group of what looked to be tourists. There was no time to be thinking about the old man now. "Welcome to Ana's Sweets!"

***

After work, Anastasia dropped by the bakery to see if Darren was there. He had told her he would be staying until closing, but the only people who were in the bakery were four men, three of whom looked like patrons. Well, they didn't really look like typical bakery-goers. They wore completely black jackets which looked suspiciously identical. Their dark baggy jeans hung low and they had sunglasses on, even though it was nighttime. The fourth man was wearing a bakery uniform, and she assumed he worked there.

As she entered, all of them turned to look at her. It seemed as if she had interrupted an important meeting. The man with the uniform looked at her impatiently. He looked young, and scraggly.

"Hi, I'm looking for Darren?" she asked quietly, feeling very out of place and somewhat scared.

"He's not here," the younger man answered curtly, in a very rude tone.

Anastasia looked confused. "He told me he had to close, because of the uh…"

"Heart attack?" The guy scoffed. "It's my old man's time anyway. Darren's not here," he said in a tone that clearly said "leave."

Anastasia was completely confused as to why Darren would lie to her a second time, but she couldn't argue with this guy, as the other men looked incredibly dangerous. She was also incredibly disgusted by his attitude towards his own father's condition. Sighing, Anastasia turned around and headed out of the bakery, not sure what to feel.

She pulled out her phone and called Darren, but he didn't answer. Sighing again, she headed home. Darren texted her late at night. *Hope I'm not waking you up. Sorry about not being able to be with you today, how's tomorrow? Please say yes.* He even added a smiley face.

Being lonely and not wanting to believe that Darren would lie to her on purpose, Anastasia pushed this incident from her mind, too, against her better judgment. She texted him back like nothing was wrong. It was the right choice, she thought.

Chapter 4

The month passed by without much happening. Darren was the perfect boyfriend, attentive, caring and romantic. Though Anastasia noticed odd irregularities sometimes, like an official-looking police badge in Darren's apartment, which he swore was a prop for Halloween, and sometimes he disappeared off to who-knows-where. But he always came back with a small present or flowers for her.

It was nice, and they were still in the cute honeymoon stage. Erica had even met Darren and approved of him. To her, he seemed like a nice boy, with an interesting job. And a gorgeous body. Erica had even begun to praise the bakery immensely, which made Anastasia very happy. Ariana and Peter's wedding was set for the next month, and Ariana's tensions were running high as she prepared for the big day.

Anastasia headed to work, a big smile on her face. The bakery had been doing well, and many patrons had said that ever since the kind elderly man in the bakery across the street had retired, his son had taken over all the operations. There were somewhat terrifying-looking men in the bakery at all hours now, and it was highly suspicious. Therefore they preferred her bakery. Anastasia worried about Darren, but she could tell that he could take care of himself.

A good thing was that Anastasia found herself actually making a large amount of profit from the bakery. It was beginning to become more and more of a valid career option, and Anastasia was really excited about seeing it go places. She had already had Peter help set up a website for Ana's Sweets, and after that her customer group grew even more. Her relationship with Darren was going fine.

Anastasia smiled and hummed a light song as she whizzed around the shop, working. She had wanted to hire an assistant, one that could help her keep up with her many customers' demands, but she couldn't. Ariana had already told Anastasia that once the wedding was over, she was quitting her job as a legal assistant. It was starting to get dull for her, and Peter made so much that he was able to support the both of them easily.

Ariana had agreed to help Anastasia out, in exchange for a share of the profits. Ariana had put a lot of hopes into the bakery, and funded some of the extra renovations and materials needed. Anastasia felt truly lucky to have such an amazing friend. But unfortunately, as the wedding was still a week away, Anastasia had to carry the weight of helping the customers and making sure they were all happy by herself.

Love for Dessert

She was still in a good mood from the bachelorette party she had thrown for Ariana. It certainly was a party to remember. Anastasia had picked out one of the best restaurants and rented out a private room. Then she had gone a little on the wild side, renting a bar, with a very sexy bartender named *Brad*. A lot of glitter, two young buff male strippers and many, many dollar bills later, Ariana had passed out on the couch in a state of absolute bliss.

The next morning, Ariana had raved madly about the party. Of course, she had to keep the strippers a secret from Peter. But secretly, she suspected for Peter's bachelor's party there had been some strippers of his own. Ariana was all ready for her wedding, and she was unbelievably happy.

Anastasia prepared for another day at work. She had sold out so many times that she was always running out of flour, and only had one day's worth left. Unfortunately, when she tried to order flour a couple days ago, they had told her that due to an unforeseen equipment failure, they were unable to provide her with the amount that she needed and that she would have to order from another company for a while.

Anastasia had decided to try out a new company temporarily, and she had used the supplier for Darren's bakery. She had seen their truck outside during deliveries, and believed them to be a

Love for Dessert

trustworthy company because Darren had not complained about them whatsoever.

The shipment was supposed to arrive today, and she waited by the back door for the boxes. At eight o'clock, on the dot, a large truck pulled up. Two burly men came out, one carrying a large box and the other carrying a smaller one. "Where's the man?" one of them asked gruffly.

Anastasia was confused. "It's just me."

The men looked at each other. One looked at his watch. "Shit, we're going to be late. Boss is gonna kill us. Go." They dropped the boxes, having no time to argue with Anastasia.

She opened the larger box to find the flour. "Oh, good." She grinned and brought the box to the storage room. She assumed the second box was also full of flour, but she had to pull it open to check. Anastasia stuck a hand in it, making sure it was the quality stuff.

Her hand hit a sharp corner.

"What the heck?" she exclaimed as she pulled out a package, surprised. It was a huge zip-lock bag, almost full with what looked to be flour. "Why is it in a bag…?" She peered at it, completely confused. Anastasia opened it, curious. It was flour, right? She knew one way to test it. There was no smell, and it was in small crystals. The flour was obviously supposed to smell like flour.

"Shit." Her mind leaped to the worst conclusion. "Cocaine?!" For obvious reasons, she didn't want to test it to make sure, but there was nothing else it could possibly be. But then this brought up new questions. Why was this brought to her?

This was dangerous.

Obviously this powder was meant for someone else. And since it was shipped inside the flour… Her mind was whirring so fast, her head was beginning to spin. *Was this meant for the other bakery? Is that why those men were there?* And then she reached the most terrifying conclusion of all. *Is he in on the operation too? Darren…?* It would explain why he was sometimes incredibly mysterious. Damn. Her heart was pounding fast, and she longed for her hypothesis to be completely and utterly wrong.

But it was almost time to open, and she didn't have time to think on that now. She got to work. The rest of the day went smoothly, but Anastasia kept thinking about the bag of god-knows-what. She didn't dare drop by Darren's workplace, for she was frightened of those men that had been there last time.

The next day, Anastasia wasn't expecting anything surprising to happen. There was no reason to, after all. But suddenly, around one in the afternoon, she heard an incredibly loud noise. Anastasia rushed out of the bakery to see what was going on. She watched as two men yelled at each other on the street, anger on their faces. It was evident immediately to Anastasia that they had just come out of the other bakery.

"What do you mean there was no shipment!?" one of them yelled, completely furious. He shoved the other man back roughly.

"Shut up!" the second one growled, pushing him back with even more force. "People are staring." They were clearly discussing something they didn't want heard. Shipment? That word clicked in Anastasia's mind. Yesterday, she had decided to leave the small bag of the mysterious white substance in the bakery. If it had actually turned out to be cocaine and in her home, it would be very bad for her indeed.

Anastasia bit at her nails nervously as the conclusion that Darren was part of the drug ring became even more certain to her. It couldn't be possible… could it? The one man she had fallen hard for these past few months couldn't be a drug dealer, could he? Anastasia cursed her "lucky" stars for bringing this situation upon her.

Darren texted her then, but she didn't answer. She was too confused about the entire thing, and scared. She knew that people involved with drugs were usually ruthless and powerful. But Anastasia didn't have time to make up her mind, for she had to get back to work. She would figure this out, hopefully, later.

***

When Anastasia didn't reply to his texts or return his worried calls for days, Darren decided that he would have to see her himself. He didn't know what he had done wrong for her to behave this way to him and he was determined to find out. So, just as Anastasia was closing up shop, he went to her bakery.

"Ana?" he called as he stepped into the bakery.

Shit, Anastasia thought as she hid in the kitchen. She wasn't ready to see Darren yet, and was still conflicted about the whole cocaine business.

"Ana, I know you're in there." And unfortunately, she knew he was right.

Anastasia sighed, and stood up. "Hi, Darren," she mumbled.

"What's wrong? Why aren't you returning my calls? What did I do?" There was genuine concern on Darren's face, and he didn't know what to do. Seeing the look on his face, Anastasia was truly finding it hard to believe that Darren was part of the drug dealers. But there was no other conclusion to make.

She steeled herself for what she was about to do. "This... isn't going to work out," she muttered. "Us,

Love for Dessert

I mean." She hadn't managed to come up with an excuse.

The look on his face was one of utter devastation as he listened to her words, praying that this was just a dream. No such luck. "A-are you sure?" he squeaked. She could almost literally see his heart breaking.

Anastasia couldn't even speak, she was afraid she would start crying. So she just nodded and kept her eyes on the floor as she heard him walk away. The door jingled as he pushed it open and left. Her heart felt incredibly heavy, and all she could imagine was his arms around her, holding her safe against his warm chest. But no more. This was for her own safety. That's what she told herself, over and over again. But it still hurt, and she could picture the look on his face in her mind clearly. That's what hurt the most.

***

The next couple days crawled by, and Anastasia missed him. Morning to night, she missed him. She couldn't think about the bakery, about new recipes, about her customers. Everything was about Darren. She kept mumbling to herself that it was the right decision to make, hoping that eventually, she would believe those lies. She swallowed dryly as she stood at the bakery counter. He was right there, across the street, yet it felt like he was galaxies away.

Love for Dessert

Anastasia attempted to distract herself by creating a new dish for the menu. There weren't many customers since it was close to closing, and she was experimenting with different types of ingredients. Quiet music filtered through the stereo speakers. It was a calm night, or so she thought.

Three men walked in, burly-looking men. They wore short-sleeved shirts, showing off their bulging muscles. Anastasia swallowed her fear, and clutched her phone, prepared to call for help at any moment. "Hi, welcome to Ana's Sweets!" she greeted them cheerfully.

"Cherry cupcake," one of the men growled. It sounded weird to hear such feminine words spoken in such a voice.

"C-coming right up!" Anastasia murmured quietly as she moved behind the glass counter, grabbing it and placing it in one of her new specially made cupcake containers. Her adorable containers for cakes and cupcakes were especially popular with the younger crowd, who frequently cleaned them out after eating the contents. They decorated them and used them to hold miscellaneous items. It was cute, and they sometimes brought them in to show her.

It seemed odd to her to hand him the small, brightly colored cupcake. "That'll be three fifty please," she said politely.

As he rifled for change in his wallet, another one of the men spoke up. "Are you the owner?" His tone was indecipherable, and seemed to be a mix of impatience and rudeness.

"I am, yes," Anastasia replied as she took the money and put it away in the cash register. "Enjoy your cupcake."

"W—" The man was about to say something.

"What kind of flour do you use? Your supplier?" the third man cut in, and the one that had originally been speaking shot him an incredibly dirty look.

"I use Tamera," Anastasia said honestly. She knew that the company Darren's bakery used was Honeymelt, and was smart enough not to mention them at all.

"I see." They didn't say anything else, and left, muttering among themselves.

Anastasia knew that it had been an abnormal encounter, but she had no idea just how important that meeting would be in the days to come.

Almost another day had passed, and Darren hadn't contacted her at all. Anastasia wasn't sure if she should be unhappy or glad of that fact. At least it was Saturday, and tomorrow she wouldn't have to work. Eventually, all the customers filtered out, and Anastasia collapsed against the counter, staring at the ceiling. But she couldn't do nothing forever.

Love for Dessert

She pulled herself out of her slump and began to clean up, wiping down the counters. She still had to pour the flour into the storage bins. And she still had no idea what to do with the packet. Sighing, Anastasia trudged into the kitchen, when all of a sudden, she heard her door swing open and slam against the back. The bells jingled furiously.

Anastasia went out into the front. "Sorry we're clos—" She was interrupted midway when she saw Darren, running towards her at full speed.

"We have to go. Now!" He pulled her arm and dragged her into the kitchen. He had a completely terrifying look on his face, a mix of panic and concern. "Where's the back door?" He was basically yelling.

"What?" Anastasia pulled out of his arm. "What the hell are you doing? I'm not going anywhere with you. What's this about?" She glared at him.

"Your life. You're in danger. Grab whatever you need, we'll go by your apartment. We need to get out of here, now," he instructed, as he checked around the front of the store.

"W-what's happening?" she cried as she grabbed her bags, and cellphone. "Tell me what's happening right now!" she commanded, but it was no use.

"No time. I'll explain later. Go!" He grabbed her hand and the pair ran out of the small bakery. He had a car waiting, and they sped off towards her apartment. He was driving so quickly, she was certain that they were going to crash.

"Why are you going so fast? Darren, explain!" Anastasia pressed.

"Hold on. We're almost at your apartment, grab a couple things that can last you for a couple days," he said as they pulled up in front of her building.

She did as he said, and was out of her apartment in less than five minutes.

"Now can you explain what's happening?" she muttered as she clutched her head.

"Yep, in just a minute." He sped out and soon was on the highway.

Anastasia scoffed. "It's been a minute." She tapped her watch and then crossed her arms.

"Sorry about scaring you earlier… It was an emergency. An emergency of…" he paused, and grinned. "Fun."

Anastasia's entire face changed from panic to confusion, then to utter disbelief and anger. "You mean to tell me… you made me completely and utterly panicked for *nothing?!*" She yelled the last word. "You're unbelievable." She scoffed loudly. "So where the hell are we really going…"

"To a hot spring." He grinned.

For a second, it seemed like everything was back to normal. But Anastasia remembered that they were still broken up. "Wait. We're not dating, I'm not going *anywhere* with you." She glared at him.

Darren sighed. "Anastasia…" He stopped at a red light and turned to look at her. "Anastasia, I love you. Whatever made you have these hesitations about us, please tell me. I will sort them out. I want to be with you. Please. Just enjoy the weekend, okay, and then you can decide. If you still want to be separated, then I'll never bother you again." Sincerity rang loud in every syllable he uttered.

Her heart melted, but she still tried to stay strong. "Really?" She glared at him, finding herself unable to say anything. They sat in complete silence for several long, pregnant minutes until Anastasia finally spoke. "W-what about the bakery? Tomorrow is my only day off." She settled into her seat, which smelled like him. She liked it.

"Ariana has promised me that she will take good care of it for you, don't worry. Just have fun." Darren's smile reassured her of this fact.

Anastasia shook her head, slightly laughing at how worried she had been that something was happening. It turned out to be a pleasant surprise. Though she had been terribly upset about Darren earlier, now it seemed like all of a sudden, it all became okay. She knew that she probably shouldn't have given in so easily but there was just something about him, that made her so weak.

Darren stretched his hand out and took hers within his. "Don't worry. It'll all work out."

They drove for another two hours or so until they reached a hotel. He stopped the car in front of a Japanese-styled place. It looked very authentic. Japanese hot springs were definitely one of her favorite things and she couldn't believe that Darren remembered that she liked them. It was a rather far place, and Anastasia was completely confused as to why he would take her so far away, when there was a hot spring much closer to the city.

She sighed as she followed him into the hotel. He was being so amazing, and nice to her, even though she knew she probably didn't deserve it. Darren opened the door for her, and checked them in. She watched him as he checked in. He kept looking around, searching for something. Anastasia thought about texting Ariana, but just as she pulled out her phone, Darren returned. "Let's go up to our room."

Anastasia followed Darren up to a room. She put her large duffel bag down, and sat on the soft bed. "Are the hot springs still open at this hour?" she asked Darren.

"Yep, they should be." Darren was unpacking. His phone rang, and he answered, beginning to talk very quietly. So quietly, that Anastasia couldn't hear him. He was peering out of the window, in a somewhat weird manner.

"I'm going to take a soak." Anastasia grabbed a towel, and left the room. She walked down the hallway, thinking about all the events that had transpired. She still loved Darren so much, but if he was a drug dealer... It was a deal breaker, no matter how strongly she felt about him. Anastasia made her way down to the coed hot spring, which was the only one open at this hour, and stripped down to her underwear in the change room. She wrapped the towel over her body, and walked out into the beautiful hot spring.

It was a gorgeous, authentic-looking hot spring pool, with steam rising so thickly that part of her vision was impaired. Anastasia felt herself relax almost immediately, as she removed her towel and sank into the hot water. All her muscles ached as she closed her eyes, feeling the water take all her cares away.

Anastasia was awoken by loud splashing. She hadn't realized she had fallen asleep, and rubbed her eyes, staring at whomever had entered the spring. Who could it be at this hour of night? "Anastasia?" She didn't have to wonder long, as Darren called her name softly.

"Yes?" Anastasia murmured as she crossed her arms. She still wasn't sure what to feel about him, and what she should do. Yes, it was a very sweet gesture, taking her to the hot spring but her thoughts were still in a complete mess.

Darren appeared beside her, in the water. "Hi."

"Hi," she murmured, not knowing what to say.

"Can we talk?" He looked at her with sincerity in his eyes, a look that melted her heart.

"I need some answers, Darren." Anastasia's face was contorted into a look that he could not decipher, and it scared him. He didn't want to lose her, no matter the cost.

Darren nodded. "What do you want to know?"

"Are you a drug dealer?" Anastasia figured that there was no point beating around the bush, and got straight to her point.

"No. But, I'm not a baker either," Darren confessed as he wrung his hands together nervously. He desperately hoped that once the entire truth had come out, she would understand and not leave him. Darren reached for her hand under the water, and he held it tight within his. "I'm a police officer. Undercover. My real name is Francis Darren Hall. But I usually go by Darren." He felt her tense up, but she didn't pull away. That was a good sign.

"So why were you working as a baker?" Anastasia sighed as she stared into his eyes, sensing his distress.

"I was placed in the bakery to expose a drug ring that has been using the bakery to smuggle in the drugs." No wonder he was so incredibly muscled, and looked nothing like a regular baker. "I'm sorry I had to lie to you so many times, I had to meet up with my handler, and I had to check in at the precinct." Darren sighed as he admitted his true identity to her.

There was a long pause, as Anastasia thought. "So what are we really doing here then?" she finally said, now somewhat suspicious that this trip was just an innocent getaway. She was correct.

"You... received a package, yes? A bag of white powder?" Darren ran a hand through his hair, his lips turned down in a frown. Anastasia nodded truthfully, seeing there was no point in lying. "Well... As I'm sure you've already figured out, it was cocaine. There is an elaborate drug- running operation set up in that bakery, with the original owner's son now under the control of the kingpin, Carlos."

Anastasia nodded as she thought about it. It was nice to finally know the truth after being kept in the dark for so long. Darren continued, "As you can imagine, having such a witness to the drug operation is dangerous."

"A witness like me, you mean," she said smartly.

"Yes… So he wanted you, to put it in his words, 'silenced permanently.'" Darren sighed as he spoke these words. "And he asked me to do it."

A chill ran down Anastasia's spine as she understood the full weight of his words. "I see…"

"Don't worry, I'm not going to do it. But your life is definitely in extreme danger now that you have been put on their hit list. Don't panic, I have a plan. I have evidence that is enough to bring down the drug kingpin. His entire ring. Once I do that, you will be safe, for sure." Darren used his free hand to cup Anastasia's cheek comfortingly. "But of course, I can't go and bring all the evidence back to the precinct. I can't leave you alone, and I'm definitely not going to take you back there with me. Our only choice is to go to the nearest police station, in the next city. As long as Carlos thinks I'm on his side, you'll be okay."

Anastasia took a big breath of the heated air, and pulled her hand away. "This is a lot to take in. I'm not really sure what to feel about all of it…" The heated air was helping with her feelings, but she was feeling uneasy. Who knew to what lengths the drug dealers would go to, to get to her? Ariana? Peter? Erica? "And… what about us?" she said. "Was that just a cover too?"

Darren moved closer to her. "Of course not. Anastasia, I love you. I have never lied to you about my feelings for you, and they will not change. I had no choice but to conceal my true life from you… and about that I am honestly very sorry. But if you are willing, then I would like to try again. You are a wonderful woman, and I need you in my life."

He was being completely honest and Anastasia could see that very clearly. "I…" She couldn't think of anything to say to respond to him, so instead, she moved closer to him and kissed him. She stood up, and straddled him. He played with her perky breasts, his lips on hers, tasting her. His tongue snaked between her lips. Both their eyes remained closed, but they knew exactly what the other felt like.

She could feel his eagerness pressing against her. "I love you," he whispered against her skin as he sucked on her neck. "So much. I promise to protect you." He left a trail of kisses down her shoulder, his hands traveling down her body and into her underwear. He played with her most sensitive nub as she shuddered against him.

This wasn't sex, they were making love. Love. She could feel it in every touch, the way he caressed her, made her feel like she was the only woman in the world for him. When he entered her, there was no pain, only pleasure. He made sure not to hurt her. As they both reached release, Anastasia felt herself drifting into a sense of security and peace within his arms. This was the perfect man for her, and she knew it.

Chapter 5

He was here. He was trying to kill her. Why? He had promised to keep her safe, but instead he was the one pointing the weapon at her. His eyes were deadly. He raised his gun, which was already cocked and deadly. He tilted it to the side. Kill shot. Anastasia's eyes were wide open in panic. Was this how her life was to end?

Her heart beat so fast she swore that it was going to jump out of her chest altogether. There was no one here to save her now. Damn it. No. Anastasia decided to fight for her freedom. She lunged at him and a shot rang out. The smell of blood filled the air.

Anastasia's eyes flashed open. Her heart still raced, and she realized that she was safe in bed. She was drenched in a cold sweat, and she still felt the all too real fear of being killed. She pressed both hands over her eyes, massaging them, trying to calm down. She looked to her side, and saw that Darren was still sleeping. He looked adorable, just sleeping there.

Anastasia looked at the clock, and discovered it was six in the morning. Memories of last night flooded back to her, and she smiled absentmindedly, remembering the fun events that had occurred in the water. They had fallen asleep almost immediately after

Love for Dessert

reaching their room. Anastasia sighed happily as she watched him with love-filled eyes.

"Why are you staring at me, baby?" He blinked open his eyes and stared at her, now awake due to the rays of sunlight hitting his face.

She pushed away her fear of the nightmare as she got up and dressed. "No reason."

"Oh, it's six already. We should probably get moving, the next city is somewhat far away," Darren said wisely as he pulled on his pants, and then his shirt. "Can you be ready to go soon?"

"No problem," Anastasia answered as she went into the bathroom, and washed her face. She got herself ready, running a brush through her hair and brushing her teeth. She then began to pack, giving Darren a chance to use the bathroom. Within half an hour, they were both ready to go.

"Alright, into the car and let's go," Darren muttered as he grabbed their bags. Anastasia nodded, looping her arm into his as they walked. They brought the bags to the car, making sure that no one was around. They settled into the seats, both ready for the long drive ahead. Anastasia was somewhat nervous, and she moved to grab the necklace she always wore around her throat.

"Ah! It's not here!" Anastasia exclaimed, surprised.

"What's not there?" Darren murmured, only seconds away from starting the car. "Did you forget something?"

"My necklace! The clasp broke last night, and I must have lost it in the blankets while we were sleeping! My dad gave it to me before he left us… I can't leave it behind. I just can't," Anastasia said, worried. The necklace meant a lot to her, and she wore it always.

Darren grimaced. "Alright, baby, let's go back and get it."

"No, don't worry, it'll only take a minute, I'll go back myself. You have to stay here and guard our things, anyway." Anastasia smiled as she began to head out of the car.

"No, Ana, I must come with you!" Darren insisted, as he grabbed her arm in an attempt to stop her from leaving.

Anastasia shook him off. "Don't worry, really!" Anastasia closed the car door as she began to walk back to the hotel room. Darren sighed as he watched her, hoping that she would be alright.

Anastasia rode the elevator as she headed to the room, hoping the maids had not cleaned their room yet. It was still early in the morning, and the sun was beginning to shine very brightly. She entered the room, and began to search the blankets for her necklace. It was a vintage-looking locket, with a picture of their once happy family all together. It was her most sacred possession, and she had to have it back.

Her hands stumbled upon a chain, and she pulled on it gently. The locket came out, and Anastasia breathed a sigh of relief as her lips curled into a smile. She stood up, ready to go, but all of a sudden, she heard loud voices.

"Is this their room?"

"Should be."

They were low voices, obviously male. And they sounded like they were heading towards her. Uh-oh. The doorknob rattled, and there was a click. There was nothing to do but hide. Anastasia crawled under the bed, and tried to stay still. The door swung open as several footsteps entered the room. She heard them open the bathroom door, the closet and various other things.

"She's not here."

"Really?" The second man growled impatiently. "Boss is going to have our heads if we don't get rid of her. Where's that fool, Tyson? Maybe he wasn't a traitor and he did kill her after all."

"No way, man. The only reason the boss sent us here was because he wanted us to get rid of them together. He's done with Tyson."

Love for Dessert

Another pang of fear struck Anastasia. Tyson was probably the last name Darren was using for his undercover assignment. So Darren's cover had been blown, and now it was more crucial than ever that the evidence he had collected be delivered safely into the hands of the police. She hoped that Darren had not followed her, for these men would likely kill him.

"Let's go look somewhere else."

"Yeah."

Anastasia smiled widely as she heard this, grateful that she had not been discovered. But as she smiled, she breathed in a mouthful of the dust. She wanted to sneeze almost immediately. But the men were still not out of the room! She tried to hold it back. She wrinkled her nose, trying to keep it in to the best of her ability. Alas, it was useless.

"Achoo!" Anastasia sneezed, desperately hoping that the men had left. No such luck. The next moment, she was dragged out from under the bed.

"So this is where you were, girly."

Anastasia didn't say a word, instead glaring at the man who smiled cockily at her.

"We can't do it here," the first man said, a rugged-looking man who stared meanly back at her. He had the oddest hair, a Mohawk or something of that sort.

Love for Dessert

"Nope. Let's take her to *there*." The second man had an outrageously large, obviously fake diamond earring the shape of a dollar sign in his ear.

Mohawk nodded, suddenly pulling out a rag and covering her face with it. "Mmf!" Anastasia uttered as she felt herself losing consciousness. And then there was black.

Unknown to the men, Darren had been unable to leave Anastasia alone, and had followed her into the hotel several minutes after. He was worried, and didn't want anything to happen to her. He rode in the elevator, heading up to the floor on which their room was. But he didn't know that in the other elevator, the men had already taken Anastasia out. They had hidden her slim body in a big suitcase.

The elevator doors opened, and Darren hurried to the room to find the door ajar. "Shit. Ana?" he yelled, pulling it all the way open, and discovered that the room was completely empty. "Ana?!" he screamed furiously as he checked the washroom, closet, and other places. She was nowhere to be found. How had he missed them taking her? "I'm such an idiot…" Darren cried out angrily.

He headed out of the hotel and into the car as fast as he could. He would find her, no matter what.

Chapter 6

When Anastasia woke up, all she could see was black. It was somewhat cold, and her nose was itching. When she moved to scratch it, she was unable. *Huh? Why can't I move my hands?* Anastasia wondered as she struggled and found that her hands were tied. Then it all came back to her, the kidnapping. Even though her eyes were free, there was no light whatsoever that she could see.

Oh no, I hope Darren is alright. She winced as the rope that bound her hands dragged across her sensitive skin. Before she had been captured, Anastasia had managed to stick her necklace in the pocket of her shorts, and she hoped that it was still there.

She was in a cramped space, and she could barely move her head. Then she realized that she was in the trunk of a car, and they were still moving. The car drove over something bumpy, and her head hit against the roof of the trunk painfully. "Ouch," she murmured quietly, as the car continued to move.

A few minutes later Anastasia grimaced as she felt the car screech to a halt. There was a lot of mumbling going on outside, and Anastasia decided to pretend she was still unconscious.

Mere seconds later, the trunk popped open, and Anastasia felt the fresh cold air hit her. She strained her ears, but she couldn't hear any traffic, or any other signs of life other than the two voices of her kidnappers. "She's still out," one of them, Mohawk it seemed, said.

"Alright, bring her into the room."

Anastasia felt herself being picked up, and there was the sound of footsteps as she felt herself being carried. A door opened, a door closed. Her nose was still itchy. Suddenly she felt her hands being untied, but she didn't dare stretch them or move. She was dropped, and she found herself sitting on a wooden chair. Her legs were untied, and her hands retied behind the chair's back.

They were just about to tie her feet to the chair's legs when one of their phones rang. "Hello?" Mohawk answered. "Hi boss. Yeah, we got her. When Tyson comes for her, we'll kill him too. Okay. Okay. Got it. We'll take care of it immediately."

"What does the boss want us to do?" the other man asked.

Mohawk growled impatiently. "Come with me, I'll tell you in the other room."

She waited, until their voices faded completely. Only then did she dare open one of her eyes just a tiny bit. After she confirmed that no one was there, Anastasia opened her eyes completely, taking in her surroundings. She was in some sort of… warehouse? There were huge cardboard containers on steel shelves, and several lights hanging from the ceiling. It was still somewhat dark, despite the amount of lights there were. This was probably their meeting place, or hideout, or drug storage place.

Anastasia remembered she had hidden the phone in her bra. She breathed a sigh of relief as she felt it there. She struggled to move her hands, but found that she couldn't. If only she could press the power button, then she could turn on the GPS. Anastasia groaned as she moved her chest around, trying to push the phone out. It was tough, but she managed to push it out. She felt it shift. Her phone fell out and clattered loudly onto the ground.

"Shit, I hope they didn't hear that," she murmured as she used her foot and pushed the phone to the front of her body. She tried to press the power button with the edge of her foot, desperately hoping it would turn on. After several repeated presses, she breathed a sigh of relief. The phone buzzed to life, showing the opening screen almost immediately. Anastasia had never thought she would be so happy to see the AT&T logo appear.

Anastasia kicked off one of her flats, and after wincing about how dirty it was, pressed a toe to the screen. She unlocked it, and pressed dial after finding

Love for Dessert

Darren's name. She couldn't hear at all, and she didn't dare turn the volume up. She saw that someone picked up. "Hello?" she whispered as loudly as she could. "Hi, Darren, please, come get me. I'm in a warehouse or something. Please."

"Is she awake yet?"

"I don't know, check." She heard the growls of her kidnappers.

Anastasia hurriedly covered the phone with her foot, glad that her phone was somewhat small and could easily stay hidden. She didn't know if her phone had hung up because of the pressure of her foot, but she hoped it was still on. "Hey, girly, are you awake yet?" Anastasia felt someone put a rough hand on her chin, lifting her face up.

She tried to continue acting like she was sleeping, but it was no use. "I know you're awake. Stop faking." Anastasia groaned as she opened her eyes reluctantly. "I hope you aren't going to scream, because there's no use in doing that." He snickered meanly. "Ain't nobody going to come save you now."

Anastasia didn't say anything, but merely glared at him.

"You might want to be less rude, for I'm the one with the gun, and you're not." He pulled out his weapon, and held the cold steel against her forehead. She softened the look on her face immediately, but

Love for Dessert

her hatred for him still burned strong in her heart. "Good girl, just shut up. When Tyson comes to save you... We'll kill him and make you watch." A chill ran down Anastasia's spine. The man was obviously a sadist, and would not lose any sleep over killing her.

He walked away, and Anastasia desperately stared at her phone, trying to see if the call had remained active. It had. "Please don't come," she whispered. Anastasia closed her eyes, hoping that Darren had heard and would not come to save her. She prayed for his safety, and that some miracle would bring them both out of this ordeal alive.

***

Anastasia quickly found out that being held hostage was a somewhat boring affair. After the first hour or so, she was growing tired of being bound to the chair. The rope was chafing her wrists, too. She let out a long sigh. The door opened, and Anastasia's head snapped up, wondering who it was. She was desperate for some kind of distraction.

From behind the door, three thugs emerged. They looked like part of the gang. They were holding large brown bags with a Chinese food takeout service logo on them. Anastasia guessed that they were out on a food run while she was being kidnapped. Lovely.

"Ah, there's the girl." One of them laughed, stroking her cheek with one finger. She shivered, noticeably upset that he had touched her. "No one is coming to save you now..." He snickered. "Are you comfortable?"

"Yes, I feel like I'm at a spa. Nothing could feel better," Anastasia answered sarcastically, rolling her eyes. She was sick of all these guys taking advantage of her, and she was hungry.

The man raised a hand, and slapped her across the cheek.

"Ah!" she cried as her cheek rapidly reddened. It stung so incredibly painfully, it brought tears to her eyes. "What the hell?!"

"Watch that attitude, bitch! You seem to have forgotten who is in charge," the man threatened. "Next time, it'll be more than just a slap. *Promise.*" He snapped his gum loudly.

"C'mon, forget the bitch, let's go eat first. Food's getting cold." His companion hit him on the arm lightly and led him away. The man sent Anastasia one more bone-chilling glare before following the second man into the room where the first kidnappers had been in.

Loud sounds began to emit from the room, and Anastasia guessed they had turned on some sort of TV. There was a good chance they couldn't hear her at all. She sighed as she returned to staring at the scenery around her, looking for a means to escape.

Several minutes ticked by, and a kidnapper came out of the room. He was holding rope, and bound her feet to the wooden chair painfully. "Ouch," Anastasia growled.

"Fuck you." He spat on the ground before tightening her bindings, making them cut into her skin even more. Anastasia shot him a look of anger which he ignored.

An hour later, she could still hear the television and the roaring laughter of the men. They had opened the door once to check on her. There was a somewhat noisy scraping sound at the door, followed by a whispered "shit!" Anastasia thought that sounded somewhat familiar, but she couldn't place it at first. She was still a little drowsy from the chloroform.

The door creaked open, and a familiar sight appeared.

"Darren?! What the hell!" Anastasia whispered furiously. "How did you find me?" She struggled against her restraints, wanting to touch him. "You shouldn't have come… they're going to hurt you. You have to leave right now!"

"But if I leave, who's going to save you?" he murmured, with a familiar twinkle in his eye that she knew so well. "We'll both get out of this, alive. Don't worry." Darren ruffled his hair tiredly. "Let's get you out of here." He moved forwards, intent on untying her.

"How did you find me?" Anastasia asked, bewildered.

"I tracked your phone. Thanks for calling me by the way, gained some extra evidence. You'd make an excellent police officer." Darren winked.

"Thanks." Anastasia blushed from the compliment. "Is that a gun in your pants, or are you just happy to see me?" she joked.

"A little bit of both, baby," he replied.

Darren knelt down, and untied the ropes around her ankles. She stretched her legs, grateful that they had been released. He was quick, but the kidnappers had tied the knots on her wrists tighter than they had on her ankles. As Darren struggled, he heard the door creak open. His eyes alert, he scrambled away behind a shelf, watching the scene. Two of the kidnappers emerged from the door.

"There's no one else out here…" Mohawk said, as Anastasia stared determinedly in a direction far away from Darren so as to not give his location away. "I doubt she'd tell us even if there was a person here."

"Maybe we should check to be sure?"

"Yeah, why not." Mohawk rolled his eyes. "I want to go back to eating though, so let's make this quick."

Love for Dessert

Anastasia listened to their loud footsteps, and out of the corner of her eye, she spotted Darren moving stealthily among the shelves. She figured he had a lot of practice doing this kind of thing, and she tried not to worry that he would be caught immediately.

"Hey, shit, I think I saw somethin'."

"What the fuck, really?" Mohawk growled. "You sure it ain't just some bird or rat?"

"Whatever it is, it's goin' down." There was a sound of a gun being pulled out of its holster. Then there was a cocking sound, and Anastasia was immediately put on red alert. She did not want to be shot, and she definitely did not want Darren to be shot.

Please let him be okay. Anastasia prayed.

"Yo! Who the fuck are you?" Mohawk yelled, and a shot rang out. *Bang!*

"Fuck!" Darren yelled out, and then there was the pounding of footsteps.

"Darren!" Anastasia yelled out, completely forgetting that she was supposed to be pretending to not know he was there. "DARREN!" She was completely overwhelmed by the fact that he could be wounded, and possibly shot. The men inside filtered out of the room, holding guns.

Anastasia remembered that her feet were untied, and she stood up awkwardly, trying to walk. She made her way to the shelves, and tried to find Darren. He stumbled his way to her side, and he hadn't been hit badly, just slightly grazed. "We need to take them out," Anastasia murmured. Her wrists were still tied, and Darren noticed this. He quickly untied her, pulling out a knife to cut through the ropes. Anastasia stretched and rolled her wrists happily due to her newfound freedom. She couldn't find some sort of weapon, so she kept her hands on the chair in case she needed to use it.

"The both of you, get your asses out here!"

"No way," Darren yelled back, pulling out his own police-issued gun. "I think I can get at least one."

"Okay," Anastasia murmured. All of a sudden, there was a loud noise behind her and Anastasia stood up, instinct taking over almost immediately. She slammed her fist into one of the kidnappers, making him clutch his stomach in pain. It wasn't enough to knock him out, so Darren turned and punched him with all his force. The man fell onto the ground. Anastasia's eyes widened in fear as she stumbled behind a shelf, hoping it would offer some sort of protection.

There were around four kidnappers left that could still fight. The odds for the couple didn't look good since the men were burly and armed, but there was nothing they could do about it. Anastasia watched as Darren shot two of them in the leg, earning loud yells of pain. He smiled victoriously, before moving forwards as if in a first-person shooter video game. If their situation weren't so serious, she would have laughed out loud at how ridiculous he looked, all crouched down like that. She even thought that he looked pretty sexy, taking out those men, as inappropriate as those thoughts were at that time.

Anastasia followed Darren as they searched for the last two kidnappers. They seemed nowhere to be found, and she was scared. She didn't want them popping out of nowhere. This room was big, and thank God for that. The shelves provided some protection, which was better than nothing. The fourth kidnapper was sneaking up on Darren from the side, and Anastasia yelled, "LOOK OUT!" Darren turned and raised his gun, shooting the man, who had his gun aimed at Anastasia. He fell, crying out in pain.

Anastasia lost her focus, and suddenly an arm snaked around her neck and held her in a chokehold. She was forced to sit back into the chair that she had previously been using as a weapon. She suddenly felt the cold steel of the end of a gun on the side of her face. That wasn't good. Anastasia tried to move her head, but the grip on her neck grew tighter. "Don't you dare try and move." The man's breath stunk, and she recognized him as Mohawk.

"Ana!" Darren called, and she watched him spin around and see her in her hostage situation. "Shit,

Ana!" He took a step forwards, his arms reaching towards Mohawk.

"Don't you dare move, or I'll shoot!" There was a pause. "Now tell me where the drugs are." Anastasia knew that they both didn't have the drugs because she flushed them in the toilet one day after receiving the suspicious flour shipment, but Mohawk didn't know that. And she had a feeling that if Mohawk found out, the following scene would not be pretty.

Anastasia gritted her teeth as she watched Darren think things through. First things first, he had to get the gun away from Anastasia's face. Darren held his hands out calmingly. "Don't worry, we have your drugs. Just put your gun down first."

"I will put the gun down once I get the coke. Hand it over," Mohawk said through clenched teeth. "Hurry up."

Darren didn't say anything, but raised his hands in an act of surrender. "I'm not going to hurt you. Just, please, let Anastasia go."

Mohawk scoffed. "In your dreams."

"Just shoot him!" a man on the side yelled, one that Darren had shot earlier and clearly was upset about it.

"Good idea." Mohawk snickered as he pointed the barrel of the gun towards Darren instead.

Darren saw his chance.

Love for Dessert

All of a sudden, Darren lunged at the man, and a shot rang out. The first one missed his body, but the second one hit its mark. Darren fell to the floor, clutching his right shoulder. Anastasia's heart was pounding so loudly, she was afraid she was going to pass out. Darren was hurt, she needed to save him!

But first, she had to make sure that the man with the gun was out of commission. As Darren tried to keep the blood in as much as possible, Anastasia picked up the chair and slammed it into Mohawk's head. He yelled loudly as she hit him with it again and again, as strongly as if someone else had come and taken possession of her body. Anastasia was very angry at Mohawk and wanted him to pay for hurting the man she loved

"Bitch, stop!" Mohawk yelled, pointing his gun at her.

"No!" Anastasia dodged to the left with frightening agility that she didn't even know she had. A shot rang out, and lucky for Anastasia, it was indeed a miss. She slammed the chair into his head for the final time of the night, rendering him unconscious. Anastasia crawled towards Darren's trembling body, her breath hitched in her throat.

"Darren? Darren can you hear me? Are you okay?" she asked hurriedly, scared that he wouldn't answer. The bullet was in his right shoulder, and somewhat close to his heart. She did spend a lot of time watching those crime movies, and she knew that if it entered his bloodstream or something, it would send him to heaven. There was no answer, and as the seconds crawled by, Anastasia grew increasingly agitated. "Please, please, please, talk to me." She pressed her trembling lips to his. "I love you, Darren, please wake up."

"A-Ana?" he stuttered out. His eyes flashed open and then drooped a little, almost as if he wanted to go to sleep. Blood was spilling out from the wound. "H-hospital. Car outside."

"Okay, Darren, let's get out of here..." Darren could barely breathe, and it was breaking Anastasia's heart watching him. Darren leaned onto Anastasia as he continued to put pressure on his wound. He could barely walk, for the pain from the bullet was so incredibly powerful. They eventually managed to get to the door. Anastasia flung open the door and felt a wave of fresh air hit her. It was now nighttime, and by the color of the night, it seemed like it was at least after ten.

Anastasia put Darren into the passenger seat, and climbed into the driver's seat herself. "Um, Darren, where do I go?"

"Just drive."

Love for Dessert

***

Anastasia drove into the next town an hour later, almost falling asleep due to the day's events. She was completely tired out, and could barely keep her eyes open. Darren beside her had already passed out, but she checked every once in a while to make sure he was still breathing. He had to make it out alright, he just had to.

She headed to a hospital, but there was barely anyone to ask for directions, and she was afraid that if she drove around in circles, it would put Darren's life in danger. Time was of an essence, and his was quickly slipping away if she didn't do something, and fast.

Anastasia almost died of happiness when she finally spotted a brightly lit white building with the words "GENERAL HOSPITAL" on it. "Thank you, God!" she murmured as she drove up to the emergency entrance. There were doctors rushing about inside, and she went to the front desk. After letting them know her situation, Anastasia watched as Darren was brought inside and medicated.

He was immediately rushed into surgery. Anastasia had never been in this city before, and had no idea where the heck she was. So the only thing she could do was wait for his surgery to be done. She knew Darren had important evidence to deliver to the police, but she didn't know where it was or even where to deliver it. So she waited.

Love for Dessert

She waited, and she waited, and she waited.

Several long hours passed before the doctor came out, even though it seemed like a decade. "I'm looking for Darren King's family?"

Anastasia looked up immediately, her drowsy state interrupted. "Me! Um, I'm his girlfriend. Is he okay? What happened? Is the surgery finished?" She bombarded the doctor with questions, for she was so incredibly nervous. She felt a little crazy with all the waiting and lack of sleep, but Darren was her top priority.

"Unfortunately, since the bullet was not immediately treated, it had moved closer to his heart. The surgery will take longer to complete, but I assure you that we are doing our utmost best to make sure your boyfriend makes it out of this okay." The doctor was obviously good at this, and used to crazy relatives. "We ask for your patience. This is just an update. Please, get some rest. We have your cellphone number, and will contact you when the surgery is finished."

"O-oh okay." As much as Anastasia wanted to stay, she hadn't slept in a full day and was feeling very close to passing out. So after grabbing her wallet and duffel bag from the car, she walked along the city, trying to find a hotel. She felt like it was a bad idea to drive in her current state. The cold air kept her awake, and pretty quickly, she found a place to stay.

Love for Dessert

As soon as she got a room, Anastasia collapsed onto the bed and fell asleep. With her last few moments of consciousness, she prayed that the surgery would turn out fine and that Darren would soon be back in her arms.

Chapter 7

Anastasia woke up to her phone ringing. It was only nine in the morning, and she had only slept three hours. She searched her bed covers for the vibrating menace. "Hello?" she said sleepily after she found it and pressed it against her ear as she rolled back onto her back. It wasn't a number she recognized. "Who is this?

"Sorry for calling so early, is this Miss Anastasia Emmott?" It was a male voice, and one that she seemed to recall from last night.

"Ah, doctor!" Anastasia sat up as she placed the voice. "Is Darren okay?"

The doctor chuckled. "Yes, he is fine. Aside from being shot, he is completely fine. His surgery was a huge success, and he is awake now. He is asking for you, actually."

"Oh, I'll head down there right now, thank you so much! Have a great day." Anastasia was in a great mood now, despite her lack of sleep. She hopped out of her bed and took a shower, making sure she looked pretty.

She was at the hospital in half an hour. Darren's face lit up in a smile when he saw her walk into his room, hips swinging and heels clacking on the ground. She looked like an angel to him. "Ana…" His voice was soft, and filled with love. "Oh, Ana." He let out a sigh of happiness.

"Oh, Darren!" Anastasia flew at him, hugging him tightly. "I'm so glad you're alright!" She cried out joyously as she released him and sat back to look at him. He looked normal, except for the IV attached to his arm and the bundle of white bandages around his shoulder. "How are you feeling?"

"Better, now that you're here." He was just as charming as ever.

Anastasia leaned forward and kissed him lightly. "I'll always be here, Darren. I'll always be by your side."

Darren grabbed her hand and squeezed it tightly. "I love you." There was complete silence for a moment, but it was a comfortable one. "Ana, you didn't get hurt, did you? The kidnappers didn't hurt you, did they?"

"No, not really. I'm okay. I'm just worried about you, sweetie."

"Right now, the most important thing we need to focus on is the evidence." Darren murmured as he stared into her eyes. "The evidence that I risked my life to get. It's critical that you get it to the police station as soon as possible, to the head officer. It is enough to make sure the kingpin is put away for life. We can save so many innocent lives…"

"I can get it to him. Leave it to me," Anastasia said determinedly. "Trust me with everything."

***

Anastasia walked through the doors of the police station, searching for the head of the officers. It was somewhat confusing to her, and she was half asleep. But she managed to find the man, and entered his office. A couple hours later, everything was done. All those months of undercover work, all the danger, everything, was done. The lieutenant promised to lock the criminals up.

Anastasia headed back to her hotel room, wanting to get some more sleep. It was as if a huge weight had been lifted off her shoulders. Very soon, the men would be arrested and her life would not be in danger any longer. It was a nice feeling. Before, at her accounting job, all Anastasia had wanted was some excitement. But after this little episode, Anastasia realized that there was nothing she wanted more than some peace, quiet and relaxation.

She couldn't wait to be back in her bakery, making people happy with her delicious baked goods. The best thing in the world was seeing those smiling faces of her customers, day after day. She was also excited to visit Darren again, as soon as she woke up…

Epilogue

"Happy birthday, baby!" Darren smiled widely as he wrapped an arm around Anastasia's waist. It was morning, and Anastasia was in her kitchen, getting a drink of water. "I love you." She looked beautiful, even though she was still somewhat sleepy. Her fluffy pink bathrobe fit her perfectly. "You look pretty."

She turned her head, planting a kiss on his lips. "I love you more," she murmured, her lips curving into a smile. "And you look pretty, too," she teased. She knew she looked like a mess without any makeup on and with her messy hair. But to Darren, Anastasia looked like an angel who had just descended upon him from the heavens.

"I have good news. Yesterday, the trial for the drug kingpin ended, and with the evidence we gathered, he was put away for many, many years." Darren grinned as he leaned in for another kiss. He just couldn't get enough. They were both extremely happy about the kingpin's verdict, for they both knew he deserved it for all the terrible things he had done throughout his reign. The baker's son, from across the street, had also been arrested, thanks to Anastasia's evidence delivering efforts.

Love for Dessert

A couple of months had passed since the terrible incident, and everything was going very well. Darren had been allowed lots of time off work, and he used it to invest in the bakery. Darren and Anastasia now both owned the bakery, and were incredibly excited about expanding the bakery since they were doing so well. Her lifelong dream was finally being realized, after so long.

Ariana's wedding had been perfect, and now she was pregnant with twins. So unfortunately, she couldn't help out in the bakery as she had initially promised. It was a huge event for her, and Ariana was having all kinds of morning sickness, upset stomachs and frequent doctor visits. But it was okay, because Darren was a great help. Darren's now famous cheesy bread brought many new customers to the bakery and Anastasia felt like she couldn't be happier.

Anastasia sung happily as she changed into her usual work outfit. "Baby, wear something super nice. It's your birthday!" Darren laughed. Anastasia rolled her eyes but did what he said. She chose a pretty red dress, and put on a tiny bit more makeup than usual. She looked very pretty, and Darren smiled widely as he saw her. They went into the car, and drove to the bakery.

Once they were there, Darren immediately covered Anastasia's eyes with a hand. "Huh?" Anastasia murmured as she walked forwards, hearing him open

Love for Dessert

the door. "Is something happening? What're you doing?"

"Nothing." Darren laughed as he led her in. There was no sound, and everything was dark.

Then Darren removed his hand, and all of a sudden, a switch flipped on and light flooded the bakery. "Surprise!" A chorus of voices called. Balloons flew and bunches of confetti were thrown into the air. "Happy twenty-sixth birthday!"

"Oh my god! Everyone!" Anastasia cried out happily as she looked out among the sea of people. Ariana and Peter stood at the front, holding huge gifts. They had completely transformed the bakery into a party room, and it was beautiful.

"Happy birthday, Ana!" Ariana rushed forward and embraced Anastasia in a tight hug. "Surprise!"

Erica was also there, with George. Erica had the proudest smile on her face, and she walked quickly after Ariana, also holding a gift in her hands. "Oh, darling, I'm so proud of you. You have a man, and I got to say… I was wrong about the bakery."

"Sorry, Mom, could you say that again? That last bit." Anastasia giggled.

"You are terrible, Annie. I was *wrong*, okay?" Erica rolled her eyes in a mock annoyed manner. George chuckled as he patted Erica's arm lovingly. Anastasia noticed, and thought that it was nice that they were still so in love. George was a gentleman, and was perfect for her mother. Perhaps this sixth marriage would be her best, and her last.

"Thanks, Mom, love you." Anastasia chatted with Erica for a bit, catching up on the latest events. Anastasia didn't mention the kidnapping or Darren being shot. Their cover story was that he had been playing with a knife and accidentally stabbed himself with it. Everyone seemed to buy it, and the only people that knew the truth were Anastasia, Ariana and Darren.

After her mother finally finished talking, Anastasia looked around the room, and noticed a long table completely full of food. In the middle of it all sat a large cake, obviously made by Darren. It had taken a long time to make, and it was beautiful. Anastasia could not stop smiling. She noticed Darren's cheesy bread among the other tasty morsels. It looked like everyone had pitched in to make something to add to the buffet-style table. "This all looks so good... Thank you so much, guys. This is the best birthday ever!" She couldn't wait to try everything.

As if he had read her mind, Peter walked up. "Try this one first," he said as he pulled out a cupcake that was held within a glass case. It was beautifully decorated, and looked so delicious. It was obvious that Darren had made it, and Anastasia was sure that it would be a yummy treat.

Love for Dessert

"Okay!" Anastasia grinned as she took the case off. "Gosh, this is really nice." She took a big bite of it, feeling the sweetness and icing dissolve on her tongue. "Oh, it's so good!" She took an even bigger bite, savoring the taste. Suddenly, Anastasia spotted a small corner of some plastic in the middle of the cupcake. "Huh? What's this?" She pulled at it, extracting a small bag out of the spongy cupcake.

Inside it, was something that made her heart stop and her breath hitch.

A beautiful diamond ring.

Darren moved forwards, and took the ring from her trembling fingers. He sank down onto the floor, onto one knee. "Anastasia, I know we've only known each other for a couple months but I'm so in love with you. I've never felt this way about anyone before. You're the first person I want to see every morning, and the last before I go to sleep. I want to create a family with you. We've been through so much together, and there is no one I'd rather go through it with. I love you so much, Anastasia Emmott, would you do me the honor of being my wife?"

Anastasia melted as a chorus of "awws" came from the women in the crowd. Tears filled Anastasia's eyes as she stared at Darren, who awaited her reply. "Yes, of course I will, Darren. A thousand times, yes!" He slid the ring onto her finger and stood up, pulling her in for a tight hug. "I love you," she murmured into his ear.

"I'm so happy right now," Darren whispered back, pulling away and pressing his lips to hers in a kiss filled with passion. He didn't care who was watching, he was just so happy that this woman was to be his, for the rest of time.

So much happiness flooded her heart, she could barely stand still. She finally had a job she loved, and a man she loved even more. Darren made her feel completely safe and he understood everything about her. She had the support of all her friends and family, whom she also loved dearly. It had been a hard journey to get to this point, but it was worth every moment.

This was right where she was meant to be, and Darren was who she was meant to be with. She finally understood why she had been through all that heartache with Aaron. She had learned so much in the past months, and grown more mature.

Anastasia knew that with this proposal, another chapter of her life was beginning, and this was one she definitely could not wait for.

What to read next?

If you liked this book, you will also like *In Love with a Haunted House*. Another interesting book is *The Oil Prince*.

In Love With a Haunted House

The last thing Mallory Clark wants to do is move back home. She has no choice, though, since the company she worked for in Chicago has just downsized her, and everybody else. To make matters worse her fiancé has broken their engagement, and her heart, leaving her hurting and scarred. When her mother tells her that the house she always coveted as a child, the once-famed Gray Oaks Manor, is not only on the market but selling for a song, it seems to Mallory that the best thing she could possibly do would be to put Chicago, and everything and everyone in it, behind her. Arriving back home she runs into gorgeous and mysterious Blake Hunter. Blake is new to town and like her he is interested in buying the crumbling old Victorian on the edge of the historic downtown center, although his reasons are his own. Blake is instantly intrigued by the flame-haired beauty with the fiery temper and the vulnerable expression in her eyes. He can feel the attraction between them and knows it is mutual, but he also knows that the last thing on earth he needs is to get involved with a woman determined to take away a house he has to have.

The Oil Prince

A car drives over a puddle and muddy water splashes Emily, who was just out for a walk, from head to toe. When she sees the car parked at a gas station moments later, she decides to confront the man leaning against it. The handsome man refuses to apologize, and after hearing what Emily thinks about him, watches her leave. The next day, fate plays a joke on Emily when she finds out that the man is her boss's brother and a prince of a Middle Eastern country. Prince Basil often appears in tabloids because of different scandals and in order to tame his temper, his father sends him to work on a project of drilling a methane well in Dallas. If Basil refuses or is unsuccessful, his financial accounts will be blocked and his title of prince will be revoked. Although their characters clash, Emily and Basil fall in love while working together and Basil's heart melts. When the project that can significantly improve his family business hits a major obstacle, Basil proves that love has tremendous power and shows a side of himself that nobody knew existed.

About Kate Goldman

In childhood I observed a huge love between my mother and father and promised myself that one day I would meet a man whom I would fall in love with head over heels. At the age of 16, I wrote my first romance story that was published in a student magazine and was read by my entire neighborhood. I enjoy writing romance stories that readers can turn into captivating imaginary movies where characters fall in love, overcome difficult obstacles, and participate in best adventures of their lives. Most of the time you can find me reading a great fiction book in a cozy armchair, writing a romance story in a hammock near the ocean, or traveling around the world with my beloved husband.

One Last Thing…

If you believe that *Love for Dessert i*s worth sharing, would you spend a minute to let your friends know about it?

If this book lets them have a great time, they will be enormously grateful to you – as will I.

Kate

www.KateGoldmanBooks.com

Printed in Great Britain
by Amazon

61812869R00088